AMISH BABY BLESSING

AMISH WOMEN OF PLEASANT VALLEY BOOK 7

SAMANTHA PRICE

AMISH ROMANCE

This book is a work of fiction. Any resemblance to any person, living or dead, is purely coincidental. The personal names have been invented by the author, and any likeness to the name of any person, living or dead, is purely coincidental.

CHAPTER 1

HANNAH DESPAIRED as she heard the silence in the living room. The occasional scratching of paper being unfolded was the only sound as her husband read the letters scattered on the couch between them. And that was hardly any noise at all. As the bishop's wife, she knew there were many things she could be doing right now, but sadness over her youngest starting school had put her in a depressed frame of mind. All of her thirteen babies would soon be grown up and gone. That was why Vera's letter had come at the right time.

She cleared her throat. "I've had someone on my mind lately, Elmer."

"Who's that?" Bishop Shroder carefully placed the letter he was reading onto his lap and looked through his glasses at his wife.

Hannah leaned further into the couch hoping he'd agree to her idea. "Mervin Breuer, Elspeth's grandson."

"Ah, that's right. I haven't seen him in some time." Elmer fiddled with his letter and Hannah could tell he didn't want to take time away from what he was doing to talk about Mervin.

"He hasn't been to a meeting in a while. Now that Andrew's settled into *schul,* I should get back into doing the Lord's work."

Elmer drew his bushy eyebrows together. "You're doing the Lord's work already by looking after our *familye.*"

After twenty-five years of marriage, she knew what he was going to say before he did and that was how she had her response ready. "I know there are lots of ways to do the Lord's work, but I meant doing what I used to do before Timothy was born. You do remember him, our firstborn?"

Elmer laughed at his wife's gentle teasing. "I do have a vague recollection of someone with that name living in our *haus* once. It might be an idea to invite him and Abigail for dinner soon so I don't forget them completely."

Hannah shook her head. "I told you yesterday we're having a combined birthday dinner for them soon." He'd had so much to do lately that sometimes he didn't pay attention to what she was saying.

"Jah, you did, but surely we can have them here before that." Elmer smiled at his wife, and then picked up his letter. Suddenly, he looked up. "Shall we have them here next week?"

"All right, if they can spare us the time, and don't forget that Michael's arriving the day after tomorrow." They regularly had visitors from different communities staying for days, weeks, or even months at a time.

"Very good." He looked up again. "And he's from?"

"Vera's community, Wiseman's Valley."

"Isn't that Wiseman's Grove?"

"*Ach, jah.* I always want to call it 'Valley,' like our Pleasant Valley. Anyway, Vera thought it'd be a good idea for him to stay here. He's been with her for two years, she said, and he's unbelievably shy. That's why I was thinking he might be a good friend for Mervin Breuer. Michael's parents died leaving him an orphan when he was a very young teenager and he's never been the same, so Vera says. He's nineteen and he needs help."

"What with?"

Hannah pulled her mouth to one side. Vera's writing had been dreadfully hard to read, but she had deciphered the word 'shy.' "He's shy. That's why I thought he and Mervin might become friends. They could team up and help one other."

"Ah, I see, two shy people together. It might work. I didn't know you had a cousin called Vera."

"I do. We exchange letters every few years. I can't remember the last time I saw her. It has to be … well … since before we were married, so I suppose it's possible I haven't mentioned her to you."

Elmer moved his letters to the coffee table. "And

you'll achieve what you want by visiting Elspeth today?"

"Jah, that's where Mervin lives."

"I'll come with you. Give me a moment and I'll change into better clothes."

Hannah jumped to her feet wanting desperately to go alone, but she didn't want to hurt her husband's feelings by telling him so. "Look at all those letters. *Nee,* you stay here. We can do twice as much if we work separately."

"I thought it would be nice to spend the time with you while we're traveling there and back."

"Denke. But *nee."* Hannah needed to clear her head and stop feeling sorry for herself. It had been nearly six years since God had blessed them with a baby and it didn't seem like there was another one coming. All that was left was to watch them grow and she had to adjust to that. It was a hard thing after thirteen children to realize that thirteen was their number. "I think it's best just I go this time, but I'll make sure I'm back well before the boys are home from *schul."*

"Okay. I'm happy with that. I'll hitch the buggy for you."

"Denke." She hoped keeping busy and taking her mind off herself would make her feel better.

LESS THAN AN HOUR LATER, Hannah was in Elspeth's

house sitting in front of the fire while they both sipped hot tea. When a draft whistled around the room, Hannah saw the advantage of her own small home. It didn't take long for a fire to warm the whole house. "How's Mervin doing?" Hannah asked, as casually as she could.

Elspeth pursed her lips causing some fine lines around her mouth to deepen. Then she pushed some strands of her white hair back under her *kapp.* "I have to tell you I'm worried about him. He can't live his life looking after me. He needs his own family. Who'll look after him when he's old?" She shook her head. "I keep asking him that. I worry about him so much at night I'm unable to sleep."

Hannah shook her head. "You shouldn't be so concerned about him. He's certainly an adult now."

"I know, but with his parents both gone I'm the only one he has."

It seemed Elspeth thought it was a parent's job to worry, and a grandparent's, too. "What we need is a plan to get him out of the *haus* and mixing with others."

A smile lit up the old woman's face. "Hannah, you're an answer to prayer."

Hannah laughed. "My cousin wrote to me about a young man who's been living with her for a couple of years. He's coming to stay with us. As I read the letter …"

Elspeth leaned forward. "Go on."

Hannah took a quick sip of hot tea and then placed

the teacup back on the saucer in her lap. "As I read Vera's letter, I thought that Elmer might be able to ask Mervin to spend some time with this young man. Elmer could ask Mervin to show him around and that way Mervin would be forced to get out."

Elspeth put her hands on her cheeks. *"Wunderbaar."*

Hannah was delighted Elspeth liked her plan. Now they just had to convince Mervin. *"Jah,* they'd be helping each other."

"That would work as long as Mervin doesn't think he's the one being helped. He wouldn't like it at all to think someone's helping him."

"If the request came from Elmer himself, I think that would be enough. What do you think?"

"He'd worry about me being alone. That's what he'd say, but I'm fine alone. He does things for me before he leaves and when he comes home from work, and as long as he keeps doing that I can manage when he's not here."

Hannah had already thought this through, knowing that what she'd just said would be an objection Mervin would give because he was devoted to his grandmother. "I'll tell you what. I can arrange for the next quilting bee to be held here on Wednesday afternoon. The young have their volleyball game at the Bylers' that night. I'll have Abigail look after my young ones after school, and I'll come here too."

"Will that be too much for you with all your thirteen *kinner?"*

Hannah giggled. "Only eleven at home now that Timothy and Rebecca are married. Abigail won't mind a bit and the boys love playing with Ferris."

Elspeth smiled. "I'll look forward to seeing everyone."

"Good then; it's settled."

Mervin opened the door just at that moment. "Hello, Mrs. Shroder, it's nice to see you. What did you say's settled?" He took off his hat and placed it on a peg by the door.

She stood and looked up at him looming in the doorway. He was the same as ever, standing tall, shoulders back, with dark hair sweeping to one side above his dark eyes. "Hello, Mervin. I was just arranging for the ladies in the quilting bee to meet here on Wednesday night."

Before she'd even finished what she was saying, he was shaking his head. *"Nee,* I'm sorry, Hannah, but my *grossmammi* isn't well enough to have so many visitors."

"There's only six of us, and we'll do all the work. Elspeth can go to bed whenever she wants. It won't be a late night." When he looked unconvinced, she added, "And Bishop Elmer was going to ask you to do something special for him on Wednesday."

Elspeth leaned over and tapped Hannah on her shoulder. "You ask him now, Hannah."

"Okay, I'll ask." Hannah laughed a little to cover up her embarrassment. Elspeth was acting a little too eager and that, Hannah was certain, had caused Mervin's brow to furrow with concern.

He took a step closer, frowning. "What is it, Hannah?"

"There's a young man coming to stay with us, Michael Fisher, and he needs a little help. He's shy and I thought you might be able to befriend him and show him around."

He pointed to himself. "Me?"

"Jah."

HE RUBBED his chin and laughed with relief. The bishop's wife was only there to ask a favor. The bishop hadn't uncovered his secret. "Sure, I'll help out. I haven't done much for the community lately." Even though his secret was safe, he sensed something else was happening here. Hannah was up to something. At first she'd said the bishop wanted to ask him something, and now it sounded like it was coming from her. Either way, he didn't care. He'd do this one little favor. It's not as though it was going to take too much time. "You said he's young …"

"My cousin told me he's eighteen, or it could've been nineteen. I know that's a lot younger than you and someone older like you could be a good influence on him."

"So, he's troubled?"

"Nee. I don't think so. All I meant was that you'd be a good friend for a new person to have."

"Denke." He didn't know that was entirely true. There'd be many others better suited, he thought. He took two steps forward. "And you want me to take him to the volleyball on Wednesday night and that's why the quilting bee's to be held here?"

Hannah giggled. "That's right, if you don't mind."

He walked over and sat down beside his grandmother. "I don't mind at all as long as that's all right with you, *Mammi?"*

"Jah. I'm looking forward to having people here. I haven't seen everyone in so long."

Mervin nodded, and said to Hannah, "I'll collect him and take him to the volleyball. I'll introduce him to everyone and do what I can to see he enjoys himself. Then maybe he could befriend others closer to his age."

"Denke. That'd mean a lot, Mervin. I could've got one of my boys to do it, but ..."

Mervin waited for Hannah to finish her excuse, but she didn't. She had boys close to that age, and that confirmed to Mervin something was afoot. Both his grandmother and Hannah were trying to get him back into going to the community events. It wasn't about the stranger at all.

Mrs. Shroder wasted no time in leaving once Mervin had agreed to everything she wanted.

Once he'd seen Hannah out, Mervin sat back down

with his grandmother. "What was all that really about, *Mammi?*"

She looked down and straightened her white apron over her long dress. "She just wants what's best for you, the same as I do."

"And, what's that exactly?"

Staring at him, she said, "We both think you should be more sociable. You're too worried about me."

He sighed. "I'll cut the vegetables." He bounded to his feet.

"No need. We've got last night's leftovers."

"Is there enough?"

"Jah, plenty."

"While it's heating, I'll cut vegetables for tomorrow night, then."

"Will you make me one of your special hot teas?"

"Sure, with plenty of lemon and honey just the way you like it." Mervin collected the used cups and saucers on the coffee table. His grandmother drank more hot tea than anybody he'd heard of. She never even drank water, just tea.

His grandmother chuckled and reached out her hands to be pulled off the couch. He put the cups back down, helped her off the couch, and then once he'd picked up the cups again, he followed his grandmother into the kitchen, already dreading going out on Wednesday night.

CHAPTER 2

On Tuesday, Mr. and Mrs. Shroder sat on their porch and waited for Michael's taxi to arrive from the train station.

"He was supposed to be here at eleven," Hannah said knowing it was well after that time.

"Is his room ready?"

"Jah, it is. Rebecca helped me with it yesterday." Their guest was staying in Rebecca's old room. It was perfect for guests as it gave them the privacy of a door leading directly outside, and there was also the added benefit of access directly into the house through an interior door.

After they'd finished their coffee, Elmer stood. "I'll do some work. Call me when he gets here."

"It should only be a few more minutes. Sit down and rest a moment."

"Very well. I'll wait."

Hannah bounded to her feet when she saw a car in the distance. "I think this is it. *Jah,* it's a taxi."

They both walked down the steps to welcome their visitor.

When the taxi pulled up beside them. The bishop and his wife looked at one another in astonishment. The passenger in the car was a woman and not a man.

"This isn't Michael," Elmer whispered out of the side of his mouth.

"I see that, but I wonder …"

The young Amish woman beamed them a smile, opened the car door and jumped out. "Hello, I'm so excited to be here. You must be Hannah and you must be Elmer." She giggled loudly. "Where are my manners? I must've left them in Wiseman's Grove. Pleased to meet you Mrs. Shroder and Bishop Elmer."

Bishop Elmer took a step toward her while the driver struggled to pull a large suitcase out of the trunk. "And, you are …"

"Michaela Yoder." The smile left the young woman's face. "Oh, this is awful. Vera said you were expecting me. She said you wrote back and said you'd have me stay."

Then the pieces clicked together in Hannah's head. It was all due to her cousin's dreadful handwriting—little more than a scrawl. It hadn't said 'Michael Fisher' at all, nor had it said 'a young man.' Apparently Vera had written that it was Michaela Yoder, a young woman. "Ah, I know what happened. You see, we were expecting a man called Michael Fisher."

Michaela took a step back while the bishop looked confused.

Elmer turned to his wife. "How could you make that mistake, Hannah?"

"I'll have to show you Vera's handwriting."

Taking off his glasses, he asked, "So, there's no Michael?"

Michaela shook her head. *"Nee,* I'm an only child. I was named after my father, who was obviously Michael. Don't worry. I've had others make similar mistakes throughout my life. Can I still stay?"

"Jah, of course you can."

Michaela smiled then turned from them to pay the driver.

"I'm sorry," Hannah whispered to her husband, who now looked slightly amused. "I can understand how I confused Michael and Michaela, but how did I get Fisher from Yoder?"

"Makes no difference," he told her, smiling broadly. "I think she'll keep us entertained."

"The boys can help with the suitcase when they get home," Hannah said to her husband when he went to lift it.

"Nee, I can do it," Michaela said. "I'm stronger than I look. I helped Tom and the boys on the farm and did the work of two men."

"Ah, so you should be able to lift the suitcase alone, then." Elmer quipped.

"Jah, of course." She crouched down, lifted one end off the ground, and then couldn't budge it further.

"Oh, help her, Elmer," Hannah said with a giggle.

Bishop Elmer laughed. "Together, we might be able to get it inside. *Gut* that it has handles at both ends."

As they carried it, Hannah walked with them and Michaela kept talking. "It's so nice of you to have me stay here. Vera and Tom thought it would be good for me to visit a different community. I like it here already, and that's so funny about thinking a man was coming to stay, Mrs. Shroder."

"Jah, it was. Vera's accidental joke." Hannah laughed again as she moved ahead and opened the door to the spare room where Michaela was to be staying. When Michaela stopped talking, Hannah spoke quickly. "This room was originally my Rebecca's, she's our *dochder.* When she got married, Abigail came to stay with us along with her *dochder,* Ferris. Then Abigail and Timothy fell in love." Another giggle escaped Hannah's lips as her husband and Michaela lowered the suitcase to the floor.

The bishop then took over the story, "Timothy so wanted this room as his own so he could get away from the rest of his brothers, but instead, he got away from all of us by marrying Abigail."

Hannah stared at Michaela. "It seems that all the people who stay in this room get married."

Michaela's eyes opened wide.

Hannah giggled again. "Now I'm the one who's joking. It was only those two. Many other people have stayed here."

The bishop chuckled at his wife.

Michaela smiled. "Oh. You had me going there. I thought for a moment that's why Vera sent me, to stay in your special 'marrying room.'"

"I'll leave you both. I've got some things to attend to."

"Denke, Bishop Elmer," Michaela said as he walked out the door. He waved over his shoulder, and when he was gone, Michaela turned to Hannah.

"If it had been true about the room, that would've been a good story to tell my *kinner* ... if I ever have any ... which I probably won't."

"Why not?"

"I don't know why I said that. I probably will someday because most people do."

Hannah then realized the words in Vera's letter must've been 'she's not shy,' rather than 'he's shy.' It didn't matter to Hannah. Michaela seemed pleasant enough and Hannah was delighted to have another female around the place. That was what the Shroder household had lacked, ever since Rebecca—and then Abigail—had gotten married.

"I'll help you unpack."

"Denke. It's fun doing things with someone else instead of doing everything myself." Michaela flipped

open the suitcase and Hannah leaned down and picked up a dress.

As she placed it on a hanger, she said, "I hope you're not too tired, because I've arranged for you to go to a volleyball game tonight."

"That's so thoughtful. I love volleyball and I'm good at it." Michaela picked up a bundle of underwear, opened the top drawer and placed them inside.

Hannah hoped Mervin wouldn't mind taking her instead of the 'Michael' they'd expected. "It's a man."

"What's a man?" Michaela asked as she grabbed a handful of stockings from the suitcase and opened the second drawer.

"I've arranged for you to be taken there and brought home again by a man."

"Oh, really? That's a little unexpected."

"Hmm, I know. I'm sorry, I didn't mean it to be like that. If I'd known you were a girl perhaps I wouldn't have arranged volleyball. You could've come to a quilting bee. You still can if you want. I don't think Mervin was that excited about the volleyball."

"Mervin? Someone called Mervin's taking me tonight?"

"That's right. He's a lovely young man and Bishop Elmer and I think very highly of him."

"It's just that I've never heard that name before. It's different."

Hannah placed another of Michaela's dresses on a

hanger, noticing it was a little old and worn. "He's a little different too, so I guess his name suits him."

"Denke, so much for having me here. I'm not sure why I'm here. Vera's been so good, but she's so busy all the time with her nine *kinner.* Even though they're older she still worries about them all the time. All but two still live at home, and she worries they'll never marry. The older two are married and she worries about them not having *kinner.* She thinks *Gott's* punishing her with her barren *dochder*-in-laws. Oh!" Her eyes went wide. "Mrs. Shroder, please don't let anyone know that. It slipped out of my mouth. She wouldn't want anyone to know I said anything." Michaela bit her lip.

"I won't say one thing." Hannah checked the other dresses she'd hung while she'd been talking. They too were old and showing wear around the seams. *This girl needs some new dresses.*

"Denke. Anyway, she's not getting any younger, and I worry about her sometimes …"

As Michaela talked non-stop about everything and anything, Hannah wondered if *Gott's* hand might've been in the mistake in who was coming to stay. Firstly, she was going to be good company for her and take her mind off her empty home during the day while the boys were at school. Then there was Mervin Breuer. Mervin was quiet and Michaela was anything but, so there was a chance they might make a match even though there was a bit of an age gap. *Don't opposites attract?* Hannah was interested to find out if it might apply with these two.

"When we finish here, we can have a nice hot cup of tea and I'll show you Vera's letter. You'll see why I made the mistake."

Michaela giggled. "I'd love to see it, and then we should write back and tell her what happened. She'll think it's funny."

WHILE THEY WERE LOOKING over the letter at the kitchen table, Abigail and Ferris walked in.

Hannah introduced them and told them the funny story of expecting a man. Of course, Ferris was too young to understand what was going on, but she laughed along anyway. She took an immediate liking to Michaela, begging to sit on her lap.

"You've won a friend already, Michaela," Abigail said.

"I have. Children always love me."

"Well, I have news. Karen's twins are on their way. I just met Rebecca on the road and she was on her way to deliver them."

"Oh, that's *wunderbaar.*" Hannah clapped her hands together. "I can't wait to see them. We must pray that all goes well."

Abigail and Hannah immediately closed their eyes and Michaela thought she'd better do the same. Once their eyes were open again, Michaela asked, "Who's Karen?"

"She's a good friend of the family," Hannah said. "She gave me help every Saturday a few years back before she married. The room you're staying in was a gift from her to Rebecca and our family."

"Jah, and she has one set of twins, two boys, and she's about to have another."

"I wonder if they'll be two girls," Michaela said.

The next moment there was a sudden explosion of noise from the other room.

"That's the boys home from *schul,"* Hannah told Michaela.

Ferris shrieked and slid off Michaela's lap and ran to the boys.

Abigail leaned closer to Michaela. "She loves the boys because they play with her non-stop."

Michaela smiled. "I can't wait to meet them."

Then a bunch of freckle-faced boys of varying heights spilled into the kitchen asking about food. Hannah jumped up and flew into action, serving milk and cookies as she introduced all of the boys to Michaela.

CHAPTER 3

MERVIN KNEW he should attend more community events and especially the bi-monthly Sunday meetings, and he'd been meaning to do it. He just didn't like leaving his grandmother alone and she wasn't fit for traveling. And it was far too much for her to host the meetings in their own home.

Although he'd concluded the bishop's wife had something up her sleeve, he was pleased to catch up with everyone, even though they would be the younger crowd. He turned his buggy up the Shroders' driveway, then jumped out and secured his horse. When he was finished, he patted his horse's neck and noticed Hannah walking over to him with a young woman alongside. Moving away from his horse, he tried to work out if he knew the young woman with the big smile. Was she one of the young girls in the community who had blossomed into a rose?

Hannah said, "Here you are, Mervin. We have a funny story to tell you."

"Is that so?" Whoever she was, he couldn't keep his eyes from the stranger.

Hannah gestured to the young woman. *"Jah,* it's not Michael at all. There is no Michael. This is Michaela."

He frowned. "I'm not collecting Michael?"

"Nee, there was confusion over my cousin's letter. Her handwriting's dreadful and I thought she wrote in her letter a man called Michael was coming, but he wasn't and it was Michaela all along."

"I see. I think."

"Hello, Mervin. I'm sorry I'm not Michael."

He shook his head, not liking this set-up. Whose idea was it? "Nice to meet you, Michaela. I'm sure all this was none of your fault. I won't be able to take you to the volleyball tonight, I'm sorry." He turned and strode back to his horse and buggy, not impressed. The whole thing was made worse by his prior suspicions of Hannah's motives. Once he had taken up the reins, he glanced back at Hannah and Michaela, who were standing there staring at him.

Now, Mervin, stop. None of this is Michaela's fault, he reasoned, figuring the blame lay with Hannah, who must be trying to marry the younger woman off.

He could see from Michaela's face, he'd upset her. Maybe, just maybe, Mrs. Shroder might've been telling the truth. He sighed, and, hoping he wasn't making a big mistake, got back out of his buggy and walked back over to them. "I suppose I could go, if you don't mind me taking you, Michaela?"

"I'd love it. Shall we go now?"

"We might as well."

"I'll just get my coat." She turned and rushed away leaving Mrs. Shroder with Mervin.

"I'm sorry, Mervin. I truly had no idea."

"It's okay." He started chuckling, seeing the funny side of this scene. Now, he was sure he believed her, because the bishop's wife would never look someone in the eye and tell a lie. He'd much prefer taking a pretty girl to the volleyball than a shy man called Michael. "I thought you were trying to match-make me."

"*Nee.* Well, not match-make in a romantic way, but I had hoped you and the man I thought was coming might strike up a friendship. Never did I think for a moment there'd be this mistake." She hung her head looking a little embarrassed.

"There's no harm done."

"I upset you, it looked like."

"Nah, don't worry about me. I thought I was being railroaded, that's all." He took a step toward her. "Sometimes I have a sudden temper."

"We all do in certain circumstances, I'm sure."

"Nice of you to say that." He looked over at the house to see where Michaela was.

"It makes no difference to us having a woman stay. I prefer another female about the place with all my boys. A young woman is a welcome change, and I'm sure you'd much rather take Michaela than a man." She chuckled.

IN THE GUEST ROOM, Michaela threw all her clothes up in the air, and then found her coat on the bed under everything. Even though Hannah had helped her unpack, her clothes were now all muddled up from finding something to wear minutes earlier. She didn't like any of her clothes and she was sure her dress was going to be the ugliest one there tonight. Michaela had noticed that Hannah and Abigail's dresses were well-sewn. Had they noticed her shabby clothes? All her dresses were Vera's *dochder's* hand-me-downs and were now years old. She'd asked for fabric for a new dress every birthday and Christmas, but it was the same answer every time. A new dress would be a waste when there were so many dresses that didn't fit Vera's daughters anymore. *Waste not want not,* Vera always said, and *It's like throwing away your money.*

She'd had a shower and cleaned up, and hadn't wanted to wear the same clothes she'd been traveling in. Once she had her coat draped over her arm, she peeped out the window at Mervin. He had a friendly face, she decided, but a little too much hair covered his forehead. What he needed was a good haircut—or a bad one, or any kind of a one. She hadn't been able to find out much from Hannah about him except he was devoted to his grandmother. To Michaela, he sounded like a man with a good heart. What did he think of her?

Pushing on the door, she headed out of the room. "Here I am. I couldn't find my coat." Once she had their attention, she held it up in the air. "But then I did. I found it. I finally found it under everything."

He nodded. "Let's go." He then said to Hannah, "We won't be late."

"That's okay. I'm going to your *grossmammi's haus* for the quilting bee."

"Ah, that's right. There are ladies there already."

"I should hurry. I'll be home by the time you get back, Michaela."

"It's okay if you're not. I know where everything is." Michaela stepped up into the buggy, excited to be going with a young man so highly recommended by the bishop and his wife.

CHAPTER 4

Once Mervin had turned his buggy onto the road, she had a better chance to study him. His shoes were a little dusty and dirty, yet his black hat was free of any specks of dust. Her attention turned to his hands, which were large and strong. She much preferred men who were taller than she was. So far, he was getting mostly pluses and barely any minuses. The only negatives were his shoes and the empty soda can she'd noticed in the back, which showed he might be an untidy person but, much like his hair, those were things that could be easily fixed.

Since he wasn't talking, she had to fill the emptiness. "It's kind of you to take me. They tell me I should meet the other young people, but I really don't want to. I do, I mean, but not tonight when I've only just arrived. I'm tired. That's why they sent me here, I think. Everyone's so nice. All the Shroder boys are really nice and then I've met Abigail and her *dochder,* Ferris. I should meet Rebecca tomorrow. Rebecca is their only *dochder.*"

When she drew a breath, he asked, "Where do you live?"

"Here, there, and everywhere since I was twelve and my parents were killed. I didn't have a regular family take me in. I lived at different places all the time. I lived the last two years with Hannah's cousin, Vera, in Wiseman's Grove."

He shifted uncomfortably in his seat. "I'm sorry to hear that. That must be hard for you."

"Why? What have you heard about Wiseman's Grove?"

He glanced over at her. *"Nee,* I mean hard about your parents being killed and then living in different places."

"Oh." She laughed. "Not at all. I've had a roof over my head and food in my tummy. That's all I need. Anyway, I think Vera wanted to get rid of me. My father died from food poisoning. At least, that's what the doctor said. Then my mother died when she went to the hospital after she had a breakdown over him dying and they gave her the wrong medication. They even admitted it. The bishop said to forgive, but I didn't want to. He said it was part of *Gott's* plan."

"That would've been hard for you."

"Yeah, it was at the time. First *Dat* going and then *Mamm.* I've been happy enough everywhere I've lived.

When I go to a new place, I don't see it as scary I see it as an adventure." She didn't want to admit to crying herself to sleep from loneliness. No one wanted to hear that. It made them too uncomfortable. From her experience, people only ever truly cared about themselves. "What's your story, Mervin?"

He glanced over at her once more. "What do you mean?"

"Why did they choose you to take me to the volleyball? I could've gone with the Shroder boys. They left already about five minutes before you came."

His lips twisted in what Michaela thought was amusement, and then he repeated, "Why did they choose me to take you to volleyball?"

"Jah." She nodded. "I could see you were reluctant to take me when you thought I would have been Michael, and you weren't happy at all to see I was a girl."

He laughed. "I thought they were trying to set me up with you, that's all. It was nothing personal. Nothing against you."

She giggled. "Maybe they are."

He glanced over at her. "Possibly, but I think they were simply trying to get me out of the *haus* more. That's what they told me about Michael, who was going to be visiting them. They said he was quiet, and shy, and … all that."

"Mrs. Shroder got a shock when I turned up. It's Vera's writing that was the problem. Hannah showed me the letter and we laughed about it. I could barely read it myself. Her writing was much worse than usual. She must've been in a hurry."

His eyebrows pinched together. *"Jah,* but in the letter, wouldn't the cousin have referred to you as he or she?"

"I guess that's true, but you haven't seen how bad her writing is. I could barely read it and I'm used to seeing it. She wrote shopping lists for me all the time. She must've been in a great rush. A rush to get rid of me, maybe."

"Jah, you said that already."

"Well, I said it again in case you didn't hear it the first time." She giggled loudly.

Again, it was silent in the buggy, and silence always made her uneasy. After a couple of moments of giving him a chance to continue the conversation, she asked, "Anyway, why don't you?"

"Why don't I what?"

"Get out. You said they were trying to get you out, or something."

"I'm looking after my *grossmammi."* He sighed. "My folks have gone too."

"Oh." She looked at the passing scenery, keeping back tears. Was he horribly lonely as well? Probably not since he had his grandmother. If only she'd had one. "How long have they been gone?"

"Five years ago, my *vadder* died and then my *mudder* left the community. I have no idea where she is because she's never bothered to contact me. I don't even know if she's alive or dead. I have no phone number and no address for her."

"Oh," she said again. "And is it your *mudder's mudder* you're looking after or your *vadder's?*"

"My *Dat's mudder.*"

"I'm sorry to hear they've gone and your *mudder* hasn't contacted you. It must be an awful feeling that she's out there somewhere. I mean, is she okay? Has something bad happened to her? It must prevent you from sleeping at night."

He shrugged. "It's just how things are."

She studied his profile as he stared at the road, wondering if he was covering the hurt of being abandoned. Even though he had been an adult, it would still hurt. "I appreciate you taking me out tonight. Will your *grossmammi* be alright by herself?"

He chuckled. "Hannah, ever the organizer, arranged a quilting bee at *Mammi's haus.* She's not alone. I've been assured someone will stay with her until I get back, so we best not have a late night."

"That's right. That's where Hannah said she was going. Your *grossmammi's* ill, is she?"

"*Nee,* she's not got any kind of sickness that we know of, but she's not strong. I've been thinking, since Vera is Hannah's cousin, wouldn't Hannah have known about you? That you were living with her?"

"They're not that close. Vera said she hadn't heard from Hannah in some time. She said Hannah must have been too busy with all her *kinner.*"

"I see."

"Where do you work and what do you do? And, what do you do in your spare time? Do you have hobbies?"

He pressed his lips together and moved the reins into one hand. His free hand went up to massage his temples. "I'm sorry, Michaela, but I've got a bit of a headache. Do you mind if we stop talking for now? We'll be there in a minute."

"Oh, okay. I'm sorry." And that was where the conversation ended. Was looking after his grandmother his excuse to hide away from the world? He certainly had no topics of conversation and had made no effort in that regard. He seemed a little rude the way he didn't answer all her questions. If she'd kept quiet they would've spent the whole journey to the Bylers' *haus* in silence.

CHAPTER 5

Mervin thanked God when they reached the Byler place. He couldn't wait for Michaela to get out of his buggy. He'd never met anyone who could talk so much and it made him tense. Even with having just met her, she'd insisted on knowing every last aspect of his life.

As was his duty, he took her around and introduced her to everyone, and he noticed she wasn't so lively around a large group of people, and she didn't keep asking endless questions. He was obliged to stay close so she'd have someone around she knew, at least a little.

Everyone was nice to Michaela, and most of them were her age. Mervin was probably the oldest one there except for Kelvin, who appeared to be the organizer. At first, she refused to join in with the games, but in the end, Mervin had managed to talk her into playing the last two by saying he'd be on her team. They'd lost both games and each time it'd been her fault for bouncing the ball directly into the net, losing them the last points.

"Come and sit with us, Michaela," Wendy Byler said, when the refreshments were being served. There was only a choice of tea, coffee, or soda for drinks, and several kinds of cookies.

Michaela glanced over at Mervin, who was talking to another man. *"Denke.* I will next time. I told Mervin I'd sit with him."

"Nee, come sit with me." She pulled on Michaela's arm nearly toppling her over.

"Oh, okay." Michaela giggled as she went with her.

Once they were seated, Wendy said, "Someone told me you're staying with the bishop, is that right?"

"Jah, it is. I only arrived today and Mrs. Shroder had arranged for me to come here. It was nice of her to do that."

"Only today? From where?"

"A tiny community you've probably never heard of. It's near Wiseman's Grove."

"Yep, you're right. I've never heard of it. Have you met all the Shroder boys yet?"

It was then that Michaela knew this was more than just a casual conversation. It was obvious Wendy was interested in one of Bishop Elmer's sons. There was no point dancing around the issue. "Which one do you like?"

"How did you guess?" Wendy laughed.

"It wasn't too hard. It was the way you smiled."

Wendy put her head down and giggled. "The second oldest boy, Aedan."

"I'm not sure which one that is. There are three about my age."

"It'll be one of them." Wendy looked around. "There he is. That one there with those two boys. There is a group of three of them over there." She nodded her head and Michaela turned around and saw a group of three young men. "He's the tall one," Wendy told her.

Michaela had a good look so she'd remember him. "The one next to him is one of the Shroder boys too, isn't he?"

"That's right."

"*Jah,* I thought he looked familiar." Michaela shook her head. "I have no idea how I'm going to remember all the names."

"Are you just on vacation?"

Michaela licked her lips. "I'm not really sure." She fiddled with the strings of her *kapp* wondering where she'd go from here. She didn't even know if she'd be welcome back at Vera's place, or had she handed her over to Hannah?

"Oh, look at your fingernails."

Michaela put her hand out straight. "I bite them. It's a bad habit I know, but I can't stop it."

"I used to do it, but my *mudder* slapped me on my head every time she saw me doing it, and that stopped me."

"Ouch! I'm sure I'll stop eventually. Vera said I'd grow out of it."

"Who's Vera?"

"The woman I used to live with."

"Is she a relative?"

"It's kind of hard to explain. She's not related. I have no relatives at all. I know that's strange. Everyone else has a bunch of cousins and so many siblings." Michaela noticed that Wendy kept glancing in Aedan's direction, and that led Michaela to wonder whether Wendy was seriously interested in anything she had to say. Was she befriending her only because of Aedan?

"Tell me."

When Wendy stared at Michaela, Michaela gave her the benefit of the doubt. "Vera is Hannah Shroder's cousin, and the best and easiest way to explain it is to say that she's someone who took me in. She's an old woman who has grown-up children, but most of them are still at home although two are married now, just like Hannah I suppose, but she has no younger ones like Hannah. More than anything she wants *grosskinner* and she hasn't got any yet."

"Why is it always the way? It seems if you really want something it's always just out of reach."

"Is that right? I haven't noticed." Michaela figured she was talking about Aedan again.

"Can I visit you on the weekend if you don't have other plans?"

"Sure, but I don't know if Mrs. Shroder has arranged other things for me to do."

"I'll stop by and see if you're home, then."

"Denke, I'd like that."

"We should be friends while you're here and then we can be pen pals when you go back home."

Michaela was delighted that someone wanted to be her friend. "I'd like that."

"Come with me and I'll introduce you to the girls."

"Mervin introduced me to everyone already."

"Did he?"

Michaela nodded. "I think you were still in the *haus* at the time."

"Probably helping bring out the tea and coffee, and all that."

Mervin then beckoned Michaela over.

"I think Mervin wants me to go home now."

"Okay. I'll see you on Sunday if I don't' see you before."

"Jah, bye." She walked over to Mervin, hoping his guard was down now that they'd relaxed and had some fun.

"Ready to go home?"

"Jah, if you are. Or, do you want to have something to eat first?"

"Nee, but I can stay if you want."

By his warm smile, she knew he hadn't meant to

upset her when he'd asked her to stop talking. "I'd rather go. I'm tired from my journey today."

"Ah, that was only today, wasn't it?"

She nodded. "It was and I'm so tired, that's why I wasn't that interested in coming out tonight, but Hannah had it all arranged."

"Well, let's go."

As they were walking to the buggy, Michaela turned to her new friend she'd made, and waved. Wendy beamed a smile at her and waved back.

"I hope you had a good time tonight."

"I did. There's so many more people here than in my community. Back there, there's only one girl my age and we don't get along too well."

"Perhaps you should move if there's nothing holding you there?"

They both climbed into the buggy. "That's something I've been thinking about, starting as soon as I arrived," Michaela said. "I like it here. There's a new feel in the air. An excited kind of a feeling. I can't explain it. Back home, the air is heavy and a little depressing. Here, it's lighter and brighter."

He said nothing further; he merely picked up the reins and moved the horse away from the row of buggies.

On the way home, she was too scared to say very much in case he silenced her again. But, he had suggested she move there, so she took that as a sign he didn't dislike her too much.

In the middle of the silence, Mervin finally said, "I'm a little too old to go to those young people's events. It's good fun, though."

"You're not too old."

He chuckled. "Men my age are married already. Mostly it's the single people who attend."

"And the people like you who are taking visitors."

"I guess so."

That was the last thing spoken before they arrived back at the bishop's house. As she climbed down, she said, *"Denke* for taking me. I had a lot of fun and I think I'll take up your suggestion."

"About?"

"Moving here."

His eyes grew wider. "Ah, that."

"Gut nacht, Mervin. Oh, did you want to come inside?"

"Nee denke. It's late. I should go."

"Okay, bye."

"Gut nacht, Michaela."

Michaela peeped in the kitchen window of the Fullers' house and saw no one around, so she made her way around the corner of the house to her room. She turned the doorhandle, flicked on the overhead gaslight, and then kicked off her shoes. In front of her was all the mess she'd left when she'd been looking for her coat. Face first, she flopped on top of the pile of clothes, exhausted from the long trip. Going out tonight was something she could've done without.

She rolled onto her back and looked up at the ceiling trying to recall the names of all the people she'd met in the last few hours. Apart from Wendy and Mervin, she could barely remember any others.

Pushing all her clothing onto the floor, she slipped between the sheets, still fully clothed. Within minutes, she fell asleep with the gaslight still beaming above her.

MERVIN HAD WAITED until she got inside the house and then he drove away hoping she didn't think he, in particular, had wanted her to stay in Pleasant Valley. She could've misunderstood his simple comment; he hadn't thought it through before it rolled off his tongue. Now she might very well tell people he'd asked her to stay.

CHAPTER 6

On Thursday morning, news came to the Shroder household that Karen's twins had been born—a boy and a girl, Cameron and Camille. For most of Thursday and Friday, Michaela was left alone while Hannah helped out at Karen's house. Michaela was determined to make herself useful, and she worked hard cleaning the house and was even in charge of looking after the boys when they came home, which meant giving them snacks and stopping a squabble or two. She'd even cooked the large evening meals on both nights.

It wasn't until Saturday that Hannah stayed home with Michaela and she heard all about the twins.

On Saturday afternoon, Michaela helped Hannah make apple pies. The apples had been canned previously, so there was no peeling or coring to be done. Michaela hadn't even heard anything when Hannah moved to the window, pulled the curtain aside and looked out.

"It's Wendy Byler." Hannah turned to Michaela. "Did you meet her the other night?"

"Jah, I did. Oh, I forgot she said she might stop by. Do you mind?"

"Nee. You can have your friends here whenever you want. Go see her. We've nearly finished here anyway."

"Are you sure?"

Hannah nodded. "Go on."

Michaela wiped her hands on a dishtowel. *"Denke."* Then she ran out to meet Wendy. She got there as Wendy was tying up the reins. *"Wie gehts,* Wendy?"

"Fine." Wendy looked over at the house.

Michaela knew she was looking for Aedan. "The boys have gone somewhere."

"Where?"

Michaela shrugged her shoulders. "Fishing I think. That's what they were talking about."

Wendy nodded, looking glum.

"Should we go for a walk? We might come across them. They headed that way." She nodded her head to the left.

Wendy giggled. "Okay."

"I'll just tell Hannah where we're going." Michaela hurried into the house while Wendy waited outside. Sure enough, she had come to see Aedan, but Michaela was pleased to have someone to talk with.

Throughout the two-mile walk that followed, they

didn't come across the Shroder boys at all. It didn't matter, though because they'd had a good conversation and had gotten to know each other better. By the time they came back they were allowed to sample a portion of one of Hannah's apple pies, and Michaela had made a real friend—and that was one more friend than she'd had at Wiseman's Grove.

A FEW DAYS LATER, when Michaela was helping Hannah clean the house, she wondered again exactly what Vera had told Hannah. No one had said how long she'd be there. Was this truly Vera's way of getting rid of her? Soon, she'd probably have to get a job and fend for herself and Vera most likely wanted her to do that in Pleasant Valley. "Did Vera say how long I'm to be here?"

"*Nee,* she didn't. Have you had enough of us already?"

Michaela giggled. "It's the opposite."

"Stay forever as far as I'm concerned. The *haus* was so quiet before you came, and now it's back to normal. I love having you here."

Michaela was shocked to hear those words from someone who'd only known her for days. She turned so Hannah wouldn't see the tears brimming in her eyes. It was a welcome change to be wanted. Even though she'd been so long at Vera's house, she'd always felt as though she was in the way and not truly wanted.

"What's the matter?"

Michaela felt a soft hand on her shoulder. "It's nothing. Just a bit of a cold coming on, I think."

Hannah moved in front of her. "You're crying. What's wrong?"

She couldn't tell Hannah the true problem. It was pitiful to feel so unwanted and wretched. "It's just that …" She thought quickly about something that Hannah might believe she'd be sad over. Mervin jumped into her mind. "I haven't seen Mervin again since the volleyball night."

"You're in love with him."

"Ah … er … *nee,* I don't think I am. I only met him the once. It's just I'm surprised, because I thought we got along. I found him intriguing and I wanted to get to know him better, but it didn't happen. He wasn't even at the Sunday meeting."

Hannah folded her arms, and stated, "And he hasn't contacted you since."

Michaela nodded, not comfortable with her exaggeration about Mervin, but anything was better than revealing the hurt inside.

"Can I suggest you take a casserole over to him?"

"I couldn't. That would be way too obvious."

"We can take it together. We'll visit him and Elspeth, okay?"

"Jah, I'd like to, but won't he be at work?"

"Ah, I forgot about that. We could go Sunday afternoon. I'd be surprised if he's not home then."

"Can Bishop Elmer spare you? I know you'll have so many visitors over the weekend."

"I'll tell him where I'm going. Helping you is just as important as helping someone else."

"I never thought of that. *Denke,* Mrs. Shroder, and … *jah,* I'd really like to see him again." And she would, that much was true, but it would've been better if he'd come to see her. He hadn't, and that could only mean he wasn't interested.

"Do you need a new dress?"

Michaela opened her mouth, not knowing what to say.

"I'm only asking because I have some spare fabric. I don't like things going to waste. You're pretty small. There'd be plenty for a dress. We could make it together."

"Oh, I'd love that. Is it truly spare?"

"Jah, it is. And, I reckon we could have it made by Sunday."

Michaela nodded. "That would be truly and magnificently stupendously *wunderbaar."*

CHAPTER 7

THE FOLLOWING weekend on Saturday afternoon, Hannah and Michaela made a huge casserole. Enough for Saturday and Sunday night's dinners, as well as enough to take to Mervin's house the next day.

It was mid-afternoon Sunday when Michaela, feeling good in her brand new light gray dress, traveled to Mervin's house hugging a potful of bacon and bean casserole while Hannah drove the buggy. "I only hope he's home."

"He should be, I don't think he goes out much for visiting. He won't leave his *grossmammi* alone except for work."

When they got there and knocked on the door, Elspeth opened the door and looked delighted to see them, and even more pleased to see they'd come with food.

Michaela, in her usual forthright manner, wasted no time asking if Mervin was home.

"Nee, he's not. He went out for a few minutes and hasn't come home yet. Why don't I make us a pot of tea?"

"That would be lovely, wouldn't it, Michaela?"

"Jah, I'll make it, though. You two can sit down and talk."

"We can sit in the living room," Elspeth said. "Just put the casserole in the bottom of the fridge, dear. There should be enough room."

While the two older women moved away to sit in the other room, Michaela busied herself finding her way around Elspeth's kitchen. All the while, she couldn't help thinking and wondering about Mervin. Hannah had been convinced he'd be home looking after his ailing grandmother. Elspeth didn't look so frail to her. She opened the gas-powered fridge and placed the pot on the bottom shelf.

When the tea was made, Michaela set it on a tray with cups and saucers and took it out to the living room, placing it on the coffee table in front of the ladies. Michaela was determined to find out all she could about Mervin. Surely Elspeth would know where he was, but she wasn't letting on. It would be interesting to learn what he did away from home in his spare time.

"I hope he comes back soon. It would be nice for you to see him again, Michaela," Elspeth said.

"*Jah,* it would."

Elspeth sipped her tea and Michaela noticed the old lady had a steady hand.

Then Elspeth looked directly at Michaela. "He had a good time when he took you to the volleyball."

Michaela gulped. "Did he say that?"

"Not with words." Elspeth smiled making her look even more friendly.

With a grandmother that nice, Michaela knew Mervin had to be a good person.

MERVIN WOKE when he heard muffled voices coming from downstairs. He'd sneaked out last night and had only gotten home in the early hours.

Who's here?

He listened hard and recognized the voice of the person doing all the talking. It was unmistakably Michaela. When he heard Hannah's voice, he jumped out of bed and pulled on his black trousers. As he did up the fastenings of his shirt, he froze. He'd heard his name mentioned. He opened his door slightly to listen.

"He likes his fresh bread, but I haven't been able to make it for him because I can't hold things with my hands. Every Tuesday morning, he gets fresh warm bread for us. I can't bake or cook anymore. I can do some things, but I can't chop vegetables. I wait for Mervin to get home and he does them for me. We're a good team, but I do wish he'd mix in with others better."

"I could make you both bread. I love baking," said Michaela.

"*Nee*, he doesn't like anyone doing anything for us."

"Why ever not?" he heard Hannah ask.

"He's like his *vadder*. Stubborn."

The women giggled, and then Michaela said, "Tell us more about him."

That didn't sit well with Mervin. He valued his privacy and didn't want anyone poking about in his life.

"He looks after me very well, but he's gone from sunup to sundown. I could tell you some things I've been concerned about."

He had to get downstairs before his grandmother started to blab too much about him. He flung open the door and hurried down the stairs doing up the last of his shirt fastenings.

CHAPTER 8

ELSPETH LOOKED surprised to see him. "Here you are, Mervin. I thought you were out again."

"As you can see I'm not. And there's no need for you to be worried about anything, *Mammi.*" He nodded to Hannah and Michaela. "Hello, to the both of you, and goodbye. I'm afraid I'm going to have to ask you both to leave this *haus.*"

Michaela's mouth opened, and she looked at Hannah who, judging by her face, was equally as shocked. Elspeth pressed her lips together keeping quiet.

"We'll go. Sorry to bother you, Mervin. It won't happen again." Hannah stood. "I'll see you again soon, Elspeth."

Elspeth pushed herself to her feet. "Mervin, you seem a little upset?"

He ran a hand through his dark mop of unruly hair. "I don't like being talked about."

Michaela said, "It wasn't in a bad way."

"Bye, everyone." Hannah put her hand behind Michaela's elbow and guided her to the front door. Mervin rushed in front of them to open it. "I'm sorry, Mervin." Hannah said, and then they continued to the buggy. As they climbed in, they heard the front door shut.

MICHAELA SAT in the front seat of the buggy, upset. Mervin hadn't even looked at her enough to notice her new dress. "Well, that was deeply embarrassing. I haven't seen someone that cranky for a long time. He didn't yell, but I could feel his rage. It was just like when I was staying at William Brenner's house and burned the huge Christmas turkey. It wasn't my fault. I was playing with the new puppy outside and completely forgot the time."

Hannah took up the reins. "Don't worry, some people just can't be helped. I learned that a long time ago. It's sad."

"Are you gonna give up on him just like that?"

Hannah's mouth turned down slightly at the corners. "What would you have me do?"

"I don't know, but something. It's quite understandable how he was angry with us all talking about him as though he had some kind of problem. I mean, he had to be deeply upset and disturbed to throw you out of the *haus*. You are the bishop's *fraa*."

"Well, he does have a problem. You can't help people who don't want to be helped, Michaela."

Michaela looked back at Mervin's house as it became smaller. There was a way to reach him ... she just knew it.

Hannah broke through her thoughts. "Maybe he just doesn't like people."

"We got along fine the other night, and everyone liked him. I could tell."

"There have been reports that he barely talked to anyone when he was there."

"But, he talked to me. *Nee,* wait, that's not true because I saw him speaking to people when he was introducing me."

"He had to be nice to you at the volleyball considering how rude he was when he met you."

Michaela remained quiet and didn't voice her opinion again because it seemed Hannah had her mind made up about him. She certainly didn't want to tell Hannah how Mervin had asked her to be quiet and stop talking. "Where does Mervin work?"

"He used to work for David, one of his *onkels,* and I don't know if he's still there or not. I'm sorry, Michaela, it was a silly idea that we go there. Just forget about him. There are a lot more men around here."

"*Nee*, it wasn't a silly idea. Not at all. I'm determined to get to know him better. He needs friends."

Hannah laughed. "Well then, I hope you're successful."

SUNDAY NIGHT'S family dinner was a good time for Michaela to do some careful detective work. By asking some casual questions, she found out exactly where Mervin worked. The next step in her plan would be executed the very next day.

MERVIN WORKED at the lumberyard where a lot of the Amish craftsmen sourced their wood to make furniture. Hannah was right, he was working for his Uncle David.

Michaela had tried to get there in the morning but with all the chores she helped Hannah with, she didn't get to borrow the buggy until quite late that afternoon. With directions, she soon found the lumberyard and was pleased there was only one buggy there, and it wasn't Mervin's. She wound the reins around a post and headed to find someone.

"How can I help you?"

She spun around to see an older man in dusty clothes, who was taking off his straw hat.

"Aren't you the girl who's staying with the Shroders'?"

"That's right. I'm Michaela. I'm pleased to meet you."

"I saw you Sunday last." He smiled. "I'm David Breuer."

"You're Mervin's *onkel?*"

"Mervin eh? You're looking for him?"

"I am." She was actually hoping Mervin wouldn't be there because she was trying to find out about him, and what better way than from his boss and uncle? Hopefully, the man knew something about the personal side of Mervin's life. "I thought he'd be here."

"He finishes work at two. Starts early, finishes early."

"He does?" That's not what she'd been told.

"Jah."

"Do you know where he goes?" He certainly didn't go home. Elspeth had clearly said he was gone from 'sunup to sundown.'

The old man chuckled. "Wouldn't know."

"Okay. I'm sorry to disturb you."

"It's okay. I'm just cleanin' up so we're ready for tomorrow."

She studied him for a moment wondering if she should ask him not to mention she had been there, but then decided not to put him under that burden. Besides, Mervin was already angry with her, so what would it matter? *"Denke,* anyway." She nodded her goodbye and then hurried over to her buggy. According to his uncle, he left his work in the early afternoon. What did Mervin do with the rest of his day?

CHAPTER 9

MONDAY NIGHT'S dinner with the bishop's family was an excuse for another information gathering session for Michaela. Her mission was to find out the location of the best bakery in town. With that answered, and positive Elspeth had said Mervin got bread every Tuesday morning, she headed to the bakery the very next day hoping to bump into him. She parked her borrowed buggy a little way up the road, so she could see all the comings and goings of the bakery.

Then she saw him. He parked opposite the bakery and ran across the road. She wasted no time heading to 'bump into' him. She stood in the doorway of the shop and watched him buy the bread. Then he turned around with four loaves under his arm, took a couple of steps, and then he looked up and saw her. "Michaela."

"Hi, Mervin."

"What are you doing out this way?"

"I had a couple of errands to run for Hannah."

He smiled and went to pass her. "It's nice to see you again."

She stepped back, so he wouldn't get away. "Is it? You didn't seem too pleased with Hannah and me the last time you saw us."

He kept walking, then he planted one foot on the road and spun around to face her. "I don't like it when people talk about me, asking questions about me when they think I'm not there."

She gulped, hoping his *onkel* hadn't also mentioned she'd been looking for him. "Aren't you supposed to be at work?"

"That's no business of yours." He looked down at the ground and then looked back at her. "I'm sorry. That sounded rude."

"*Jah,* it did."

"I have to go." He sprinted across the road, jumped into his buggy, and then he was gone.

WHEN MICHAELA GOT BACK to the bishop's *haus,* she was reminded, by Abigail and Ferris's presence, that it was Timothy and Abigail's combined birthday dinner that night. Abigail was there to help and while Hannah was putting Ferris down for her midday nap, Michaela took the opportunity to get some older-young-woman advice. Michaela told Abigail about going to the volleyball games with Mervin, and his actions since.

"I don't really know him. I've only met him twice, I think. I'm not from this community."

"Jah, I know that. Hannah told me. Anyway, he disappears for hours a day. What's he doing, do you think?"

"Maybe he has a second job and doesn't want to tell everyone."

"Jah, but wouldn't he tell his *grossmammi?"*

"I guess so. Do you think he's doing something bad?"

"I don't know, but ... maybe."

"Then you should keep away from him and pay him no mind."

Michaela stared at her new friend and slowly nodded, but she had no intention of doing so. "Maybe."

Throughout the birthday celebrations that night, all Michaela could think about was the mysterious Mervin. She wasn't in love with him like Hannah had once thought, but she saw in him a reflection of herself. He was the male version of her, and he was carrying his own private pain. Together, they could help one another. No one had ever understood her and she hoped Mervin might, given time. If only he'd let his barriers down and see she wanted to befriend him. If he was in some kind of trouble, she could help.

In bed later that night, she was still thinking about Mervin and wading through endless possibilities of where he was going when he finished work. Then, like a bolt of lightning on a clear summer's day, inspiration hit her.

The only way to find out for certain was to follow him. She already knew where he worked and she'd follow him from there. Only thing was, she had to do it without him knowing … but how?

How would she follow him? Hiring a car wasn't the answer. He'd notice a car driving slowly behind him. A horse! That was the best option. On horseback, she could follow in the fields without being seen, and a horse would easily keep pace with another horse pulling a buggy. But, did the Shroders have a horse that was trained under saddle?

Michaela only stopped thinking about the man with the wild dark hair when sleep finally overtook her.

CHAPTER 10

After breakfast the next morning, Michaela put part one of her plan into action by asking Hannah if she might borrow a horse.

Hannah looked surprised. "A horse and buggy?"

"Nee, just a horse by itself."

"What for?"

"I love riding."

"Horseback riding?" Hannah asked, frowning.

"Jah. Oh, I hope that's all right. All communities have different views on that. Some I've been in don't like it, but other communities I've lived in see nothing wrong with riding and even harness racing."

Hannah smiled. "It's fine. Although we don't ride ourselves, I know my buggy horse has been ridden with no problems. When did you want to borrow her?"

"Denke. Later today. This afternoon. Early afternoon."

Hannah laughed. "Okay, just this once." Hannah leaned toward her. "And, best not to let anyone see you."

She giggled. *"Denke,* Mrs. Shroder, that was exactly my plan. Which horse is she?"

"Millie's the bay with the long mane."

"I won't be that late home."

"Take your time. You young girls should do these things before you're blessed with a household of your own."

"Ah … *jah,* definitely. Um, is there a saddle?"

"Timothy bought a saddle from an auction years ago. I'm sure it's still in the barn somewhere."

"I'll find it."

"Stay there a moment and I'll get you a map of the area to stop you from getting lost."

Michaela giggled. "I hadn't even thought of that."

AFTER SEARCHING in the barn for half an hour, Michaela found a proper bridle and a saddle in a small room that housed the animals' feed. She used an old blanket as a saddle cloth and saddled the horse. With the map tucked into the top of her sleeve, she set out on her adventure.

It was just on two when the lumberyard came into view. She stayed a distance away, but could plainly see Mervin's dark brown buggy horse amongst all the horses and buggies of the workers. "I hope he goes this way, Millie, or we'll have to gallop so he doesn't get away from us." Then, she thought twice about that idea, not wanting to gallop in the paddock in case there was a rabbit hole or a sudden fence they'd have no time to stop for. For this to work, he'd have to come toward them; the same way he'd go if he was going back to his house.

Then she saw the workers leaving the main building. A couple of them stopped to talk, but Mervin went to his buggy.

To Michaela's delight, he set off in her preferred direction, and she stayed low behind a clump of trees. Then, once he passed, she stayed as far back as she could and followed at a safe distance. After five minutes, he turned left.

"He's not going home. Let's see where he goes," she said into the air.

Millie's ears twitched in response to her voice.

Michaela's heart thumped hard as she continued to shadow him. The road got narrower, and then she lost him. There was no other choice but to ride on the deserted roadside to catch sight of him again. Looking over her shoulder, she hoped she wasn't going to break her word to Hannah and be seen. Thankfully, there was no one about; not on this road. Then the road narrowed into nothing more than a trail, and ended five minutes further along. She spotted his buggy near an old building that looked like it might've been a mill in times gone by. She jumped off her horse and watched Mervin leave his buggy and walk to the building carrying two large bags.

"What's he up to?" She crouched down, then watched as the door opened and a young woman stood there smiling, with a baby in her arms. Michaela covered her mouth in shock.

CHAPTER 11

WHEN MERVIN HAD WALKED INSIDE and closed the door, Michaela tied the horse to the nearest tree and headed closer, hoping to overhear something. Was he hiding a secret lover and their baby? It was outrageous. What would she do with that information if that were true?

Keeping out of sight the best she could, she made her way closer, and then crouched under a partially open window hoping to learn what was going on. A twig behind her snapped and her heart nearly leaped out of her chest. Still crouched, she turned around slowly sensing a presence. Mervin stood there, feet planted firmly on the ground with his arms folded across his chest.

"Why are you following me?"

She jumped to her feet. "I wanted to find out what you were doing."

His lip curled, showing how angry he was. "Obviously, but why?"

"I thought you had a problem and I wanted to help."

He took a step closer and lowered his voice. "Shush. Keep quiet. Sit in my buggy and I'll be out in a minute. If my friend knows you've followed me here, she'll be horribly upset."

"Okay. I can do that." She hurried over and sat in his buggy waiting for him. A couple of minutes later, he joined her. He said nothing, but drove on.

"My horse." Michaela pointed to Millie.

"I'm going to clip him onto the end of my buggy."

"Her."

He frowned at her, and then corrected himself. "Her. I'm just moving the buggy now so Lucinda doesn't see you." He stopped his buggy beside Millie and then tied her onto the back.

Once they were on the regular road, Michaela knew she had to get to the bottom of it. "What's going on? Do you have a secret *fraa* and a *boppli?* A secret *familye?"*

He shook his head. "It's nothing like that."

She scoffed. "A lover?"

"Nee. The woman's my friend and that's the end of that." He looked over at her. "You can't tell anyone."

"Are you in trouble?"

"Nee, but my friend is if anyone finds out about her. Her life could be in danger and so could her child's."

Michaela folded her arms, not happy about not knowing everything. "You can tell me."

"I can't and I won't."

"What if I tell Bishop Elmer?"

He stopped the buggy in the middle of the road, and his hazel eyes flashed with urgency. "You can't. It's a matter of life and death. You can't tell anyone where I've been just now, or who you saw me with. You must trust me on this."

"You can't tell me the truth, so why should I trust you about anything?"

He shook his head and jiggled the reins to move his horse forward. "I can't say more than I already have. There are dangerous people involved. People who think nothing of killing. All our lives could be in danger, and ... especially my friend and her child."

Michaela wondered if everything he said was lies. Was that his child back there, and he didn't want the community to know he'd had a child out of wedlock? "Who was that woman back there and was that her child?"

"Forget what you saw. It doesn't concern you."

"Is she one of us? She wasn't wearing Amish clothes."

"I'm not saying anything."

"Come on. You can tell me."

He didn't answer, and he also didn't comment on anything she said or asked for the rest of the journey, much to Michaela's annoyance. He only spoke again when he got to the bottom of Bishop Elmer's driveway. "I'll let you out here." He jumped out and untied her horse. When she met him behind the buggy, he handed her the reins. "I urge you please, keep quiet about this. If you want to help me, be friends with me, or whatever you said, then please do it by saying nothing. From what I know of you so far, keeping quiet's gonna be hard."

"I can do it." She nodded. "I'll tell no one."

"Denke, Michaela. Remember it is a life and death situation." He nodded, and then jumped back into his buggy.

She stared after him, wondering what was going on with that woman and the baby. If Mervin hadn't told her how dangerous everything was, she wouldn't have wanted to know so bad. Then, remembering her word to Hannah, she walked up the driveway leading the horse, hoping no one saw the horse saddled.

Once she had rubbed Millie down, she put the saddle and bridle back where she'd found them and went in search of Hannah.

Hannah looked up from peeling vegetables when Michaela entered the kitchen. "What's wrong?"

"Nothing."

"Did you fall off the horse? You look dreadful."

"Nee. It's just that ..." She rubbed her behind. "I haven't ridden for a while."

Hannah laughed. "Well, I hope it doesn't hurt you to sit down and help me peel these." She nodded to the pile of vegetables in front of her. It took a mountain of food to feed all the Shroder boys and all the people who often stopped by right at dinner time.

"I'll manage." She picked up a potato and a peeling knife and gingerly sat down opposite. "Mrs. Shroder, how would I go about finding out what babies have been recently born around these parts?"

"Ask Rebecca. She's the midwife everyone uses."

"Oh, that's right. Then she'd know?"

Hannah frowned. "Know what exactly?"

"Um ... I'm just wondering if people are having as many *bopplis* these days. I mean, look at you with thirteen. Are the young women having that many? I don't think so."

Hannah laughed. "They will when they're older. They don't have them all at once you know, Michaela."

Michaela giggled too. "I know that, but not everyone has thirteen. Will Rebecca be visiting soon?"

"I don't know. She just sees us whenever she can."

Michaela nodded, knowing Rebecca was there nearly every second day and she wouldn't have to wait long. Who else would've delivered the baby if it was to be kept a secret? Rebecca was the perfect midwife for that.

CHAPTER 12

Michaela didn't have to wait too long to see Rebecca because it was the next day when she stopped by. She drank tea politely with Rebecca and Hannah, and when Rebecca was ready to leave, she walked her out to her buggy while Hannah packaged up some cookies for Rebecca's young stepson. "Rebecca, what do you know about a woman from this community—well, I think she was from this community, or maybe not, having a *boppli* in secret?"

Rebecca screwed up her nose. "Are you talking about Mary's *boppli?*"

"Mary, that's her name?" Michaela was sure Mervin had called her by a different name.

"I'm not sure what you're talking about."

Michaela said, "Who's Mary, then?"

"It's a long story and it all happened ages ago."

"Oh, well, I don't mean that then. Would there

perhaps be a child born recently that someone wants to keep hush-hush?" She watched Rebecca's demeanor change.

"You must keep quiet about things like that. Don't breathe a word. What do you know exactly? Do my folks know?"

"Nee." Michaela shook her head.

Rebecca frowned. "Why are you asking?"

"Because I want to know. It involves Mervin, doesn't it?"

Rebecca's face turned white. "Whatever you've found out, you must forget it and never mention it to a soul—ever. It's complicated, but peoples' lives could be in grave danger. It's vital you don't breathe a word. Whatever you know you must forget it."

Both girls turned to see Mrs. Shroder walking toward them. Rebecca immediately fixed a smile on her face as her mother handed her the cookies. "Bye, *Mamm,* and *denke.* He'll love these."

"See you soon and bring Micah with you next time. I don't see enough of him."

"I will." Rebecca climbed into the buggy, and then said out the window, "That is, if I can get him away from Anne for long enough."

"Bring her along too," Hannah called after her as she drove away.

As they walked back to the house, Hannah said to Michaela, "You seemed in deep conversation just now."

"She was just filling me in about people in the community."

"Not gossip I hope."

Michaela shook her head. *"Nee.* I wouldn't do that. Would I be able to borrow a buggy this afternoon?"

"Given up horseback riding already?"

Michaela giggled as they walked up the porch steps. "I have, and you said it would be just the once."

"That's right, I did. You can borrow the buggy. Where are you going?"

"I thought I'd just drive around if that's okay."

"Sure. Don't forget to take that map I gave you. We don't want to be sending out a search party."

Michaela giggled. "It's in my room."

"Go now if you want."

"Are you sure?"

"Jah. Then you'll be back in time to help with the evening meal."

"I'll be back in plenty of time. Will I take Millie again?"

"Give her a rest and take the chestnut. He's in the adjoining paddock."

"Great! Bye." Instead of going inside through the front door, Michaela went to her room to get the map. There was only one place she intended on going. She wanted to get to the bottom of the mystery surrounding the woman and the baby. If there was danger surrounding them, why were they living out there all alone in the falling down building?

. . .

MICHAELA PULLED her buggy off the road where she'd stopped last time. She had intended to knock on the door and confront the woman, with the idea being that she'd say she was new to the area and had lost her way. Not all of that would be a lie, just an exaggeration. As she was justifying, to herself, the little speech she had prepared, she heard the rumblings of a buggy.

It was Mervin and he was glaring at her. He stopped beside her. "What are you doing?"

"I want to know what's going on."

He shook his head. "You're unbelievable. I told you to drop it."

She rushed to him. "Just tell me, Mervin. Whatever it is I might be able to help. I can talk to Bishop Elmer and make him see that plenty of people make mistakes. It might be rough for you and your … girlfriend, but in time no one will remember. You can get married and all would be forgiven and forgotten."

"Wait a minute. You think the *boppli's* mine?"

"Well …."

He rolled his eyes, and repeated, "You're unbelievable. Lucinda's my good friend. She went on *rumspringa* and found herself pregnant."

"Found herself, just like that? That's a miracle that I believed only happened once."

"Don't joke about it."

"Okay. I'm sorry. Go on."

"She wound up pregnant and the father of her child is a dangerous man. She escaped from him and she's hiding out here. He's heavily involved in the drug world. Lucinda said he's a hit man—murders people. He thinks nothing of killing. He doesn't know where Lucinda is and he doesn't know she was pregnant. As soon as she found out, she asked me for help. She's been hiding here ever since."

"Really?"

"*Jah.* I've been bringing her food and looking after her."

"Rebecca knows all this?"

"Why? Did she say something?"

"*Nee.* I asked her about someone having a *boppli* in secret and she thought I was talking about someone else." She shook her head. "Your community sure is interesting, not like where I come from. Anyway, she told me to keep quiet if I knew anything, which I didn't."

"That's right. We'll all be killed if he finds out, and since you have an insatiable need to know every detail of something that doesn't concern you, Rebecca delivered the *boppli*."

"I already figured that out. Why hasn't this man already come looking for her?"

"Because he has no idea she's Amish. She met him in New York and all he knows about her is that she grew up on a farm and that she was a long way from home. Still, we're not taking any chances in case she was followed all the way, or part of the way, back here. They've got their ways of finding people."

"So, she is from this community?"

He nodded. *"Jah."*

"What will you do? She can't hide away here forever."

"I know and she doesn't want to. We're figuring it out."

"How old is the *boppli* and is it a boy or a girl?"

"Boy, and he's only a couple of weeks old."

"Aw, can I see him?"

"Okay. I suppose it won't hurt now that you know. You must promise to keep quiet. Lucinda's a little uptight and nervous."

"I will. I'll keep quiet."

"Let's take you to meet Lucinda, then. Jump in."

She got into his buggy and he drove a few more yards, then tied his horse in the same place it was the other day. Walking right behind him, she followed him to the door. When he knocked on the weather-worn door, Michaela stopped well behind him. A few seconds later, Lucinda opened the door and stared open-mouthed at Michaela.

"Lucinda this is a friend of mine. Don't be scared. She's okay."

Her mouth closed and her eyes blazed with anger. "Are you kidding me right now, Mervin?"

"It's okay. Calm down."

"How can I? We agreed no one would ever know I'm here." She scowled at him.

Michaela stepped forward and offered her hand. "I'm Michaela. I'm from Wiseman's Grove."

"It's okay, Lucinda. She's all right," Mervin insisted.

She spat out words to Mervin. "We agreed no one was to know I was here."

Michaela lowered her hand that had been waiting to be shaken. "It's not his fault. I followed him here."

Lucinda completely ignored her. "If she can follow you that easily. I'm not safe here. I'll have to find somewhere else."

Michaela said, "It's okay. I didn't see anyone else following him."

Mervin held up his hands. "Michaela figured I was hiding something and that's why she followed me. And, maybe three heads are better than one, or two, in helping us to figure out your next move. You're right, you can't stay here forever, but your next move will have to be carefully planned. Now can we come in, or what?"

Lucinda stepped back to allow them through, still not looking happy.

Once inside, Michaela looked around the dark place. It was darker and even more depressing than the room she had stayed in at Vera's house. "Where's the *boppli?*"

"Mervin, you told her about the baby?" She perched her hands on her hips, glaring again at Mervin.

He nodded. "I'm sorry. She's the only one who knows. She's got a way of making me tell her things."

Lucinda shook her head.

"Don't blame him. I followed him and saw you and the *boppli* when you opened the door. He's done a good job, hasn't he?"

Lucinda glared at the two of them. "I hope you told her how dangerous these people are?"

"I did, but they won't be looking for you in or around an Amish community."

"They have help. They even have cops on their payroll. You can't trust anyone. How do we know she's not one of them?"

"I'm not."

"She's not. The bishop's *schweschder*-in-law's cousin knows her and she's staying with the bishop."

"Actually, it's the bishop's *fraa's* cousin. That's who I was living with before I came here."

Lucinda shook her head. "I'm going to have to make a move soon."

"*Jah*, I know," Mervin agreed.

Lucinda looked Michaela up and down. "The baby's asleep. I'll show you."

"Thank you. I'd love to see him." She followed Lucinda. At first, it just looked like a black wall in the dim lighting, but there was a handle and a door, and when Lucinda opened it, it led to another room. When they walked through the doorway, Lucinda flicked on a lamp. Michaela saw a single bed and next to it was a crib. Michaela walked closer and saw the sleeping baby. "Aw, he's the most beautiful *boppli* I've ever seen." Michaela crouched down to get a better look.

"Jah, he is, but I'm not cut out for all this."

Michaela looked up at her not knowing exactly what she meant. "You've left the Amish, and you don't want to return?"

"No, I don't. There's nowhere I can go, not in this country. My brother was supposed to buy me a ticket to join him in England, but I couldn't get to a phone to contact him to arrange the next step."

"Why not?"

"I've got to figure out what to do with the *boppli* before I do anything."

Mervin walked into the room. "What are you saying, Lucinda? You'll take him with you of course."

"I knew you'd carry on. That's why I didn't tell you that's what I'd decided for certain."

Frustrated, he pushed a hand through his hair. "He's your son, Lucinda."

"Don't make me feel guilty."

Michaela stood up and walked out of the room. She'd never been comfortable with confrontation.

Lucinda added, "Eric knows nothing about a baby and he mightn't let me stay with him. He doesn't like babies."

"Eric's your brother?" Michaela asked when they both joined her in the other room.

Lucinda nodded.

"Doesn't everyone like them?" Mervin asked.

Lucinda was silent for a moment, before she said, "I'm not cut out to be a mother. I've tried to tell you this before, but you just never listen."

Mervin said, "But Rebecca said many young mothers feel like that. It'll take time."

"I've never been domestic and that's why I left." Lucinda looked at Michaela. "Do you understand?"

"Not really. Everyone's different I suppose."

"That's the way I am. I want the best for him, but he's better off with someone who can give him a family and a decent life."

Michaela hoped Lucinda would change her mind. She knew what it was like, being alone in the world with no parents. "What's his name?"

"I've been trying to think of one. I wanted to name him Mervin, but Mervin won't let me."

Michaela looked at Mervin. "Why not?"

Mervin chuckled. "It's a dreadful name."

"It might be just a little bit," Michaela laughed, "but it's a lovely thought."

"Mervin's been there for me through everything."

"Let's sit down and figure out what to do. Like you said, if Michaela figured out that I'm hiding something and disappearing to somewhere, it won't be long before other people do."

"I'm not worried about people in the community," Lucinda said.

Mervin nodded. "I know."

They all sat cramped together on an old two seater couch.

"I need to contact my brother. Either by phone or email. I don't think they'd know about my brother. Maybe Eric's not even looking for me anymore."

"When did you escape?" Michaela asked.

"As soon as I found out I was pregnant. Probably about ten months ago now."

"How long were you with him?"

"Just a year, or a little more."

Michaela saw how sad she was. "Can one of us contact your brother?"

"He might not trust you. He knows what danger I'm in and he's been waiting for me to contact him."

"You've got his phone number, right?"

"Yes."

"Why don't you come with me? I'll collect you and bring an extra set of Amish clothes."

Mervin shook his head. "If someone sees you two together it won't be good. They'll think Lucinda has come back to the community and then her family will find out."

"Isn't there a pay phone somewhere that's not so public?"

"I had to toss away my cell phone because that can be traced, but … if you could get me a cheap phone, Mervin, then I can dispose of it once I call my brother."

"Sounds like a plan," Mervin said. "Why didn't we do this before now?"

"I don't know why I didn't think of it before. That's why they call it "baby brain," I suppose."

"I'll try to get one tomorrow," Michaela said. "I can do it if Hannah allows me to borrow the buggy again."

"Why don't I collect you? If they think you're spending time with me, they'll feel better—rather than you driving off alone somewhere."

"Good point, since that's what I've done today."

"Exactly."

"I'll send you money, Mervin, as soon as I get some."

"Nee, don't worry about it. Besides, something like that might be traced. You never know."

As they planned getting the phone, no one mentioned the one thing that was on all their minds. What would happen to the baby, since Lucinda wasn't planning on taking him with her?

CHAPTER 13

As Michaela and Mervin drove to get the phone, Michaela said, "I'll have the baby if she's giving him away."

"Nee, I think she's planning to give him to a family. If my *grosssmammi* wasn't so frail, I'd adopt him myself." He sniffed back tears. "I'm sorry." He wiped the tears away with the back of his hand.

"Don't feel bad about crying."

"I was raised to know that men don't cry, but they do." He chuckled. "That doesn't make sense, what I just said."

"I know what you meant."

"I'll think about him every day hoping and praying he'll be okay."

"What if we tell Lucinda we're getting married?"

"You'd marry me for the sake of the baby?" He stopped the buggy and looked at her, not noticing when his horse began turning them around. He jiggled the reins and the horse started walking back the way they'd come.

"We'll tell Lucinda that and by the time she's gone …"

"Nee, Michaela. That's not the answer."

She gulped and shrank into her seat. She hadn't meant she would marry him for real, just to play a charade in front of Lucinda, so Mervin would get to take care of the baby until Lucinda came back to get him. Michaela had made up her mind a long time ago never to marry. She didn't believe in love. *It's all in their minds,* she thought. *They talk themselves into love.* She shook her head. "I know. You're right. There'd be many families who'd love to take him."

He frowned at her.

"I was joking," she told him bluntly.

He nodded.

"What? Were you serious? Did you seriously think I'd marry you?"

He smiled. "I thought you meant it. I'm not used to people joking all the time. I'm used to men more than the company of women."

"Nee you're not. You might work with men all day, *jah* that's true, but Lucinda's your friend and you live with your *grossmammi."*

"I don't see them as … never mind."

"As what?"

"Nothing." He finally realized they were going the

wrong way, stopped the buggy and turned it around again. "Let's just get this phone."

"Okay." She felt bad for giving him false hope. Then she wondered why he'd let the horse turn them around when he thought they would marry. Wouldn't Lucinda still need that phone either way? He wasn't thinking right.

When they got to the phone store there was a sign on the door that they were closed just for the day due to a problem with the electricity. Mervin was upset and once he had pulled out onto the open road, Michaela thought she could take his mind off things by having a nice conversation. "And, what do you want out of life, Mervin? What do you want your future to look like?"

"I've always wanted a family. A large family. I was an only child and I've always wanted brothers and sisters."

"And you'll make up for that by having a large family?"

"I suppose it sounds ridiculous."

"Nee, it doesn't. Not at all. We've both known the loneliness of being an only child. I know what that's like, but the thing was that there were always so many other children around."

"Yeah, but they get to go home and live together whereas I went home to a quiet *haus."*

"Is that why you're so quiet now?"

He nodded. "I guess I'm used to it now."

"So, do you still want a large family? They will be noisy." Michaela giggled.

"I would like that, but as the years pass it seems further and further out of reach."

"I'm sure you'll get what you want, but you really should get out more and meet people."

"Now you sound like my *grossmammi."*

"Sometimes in life, we have to make things happen. You can't just sit around whining about things and expect everything to fall into place."

He glanced over at her and laughed. "I'm not whining. You asked me what I wanted and I'm simply answering your questions."

She giggled. "Well, you know what I mean."

"Not really."

"But seriously, what do you think will happen to the *boppli?* Lucinda said she doesn't want to take him with her. Does she mean it?"

"I believe she does intend to keep him, but if not, maybe the bishop and Hannah might take him in and raise him."

"I think he needs to be with a younger family. Maybe Rebecca and her husband, or Abigail and Timothy? Or Karen, she's just had twins and he's only a few weeks older than them. They'd be like triplets."

"Maybe." He nodded. "I think there'd be a few families who'd be happy to take him, but you know what?"

"What?"

"He'd just be another child and not special. I'm thinking about a childless couple."

Michaela shook her head. "I disagree. Of course he'd be special because he'd be a special gift to them. *Gott's* special unexpected gift. *Gott's* blessing."

Mervin nodded, and moaned quietly. "I want him to be a special gift to me."

"Well, maybe there's a way he can be."

He stared at her taking his eyes off the road. "What do you mean?"

"You take him, if Lucinda agrees and I'm sure she will."

"I dunno. I can't look after him in the lumberyard and my *grossmammi* isn't physically capable."

"You could employ somebody to look after him while you're at work. I'll help out."

"Denke for the offer. I have considered doing that and maybe that's what I should do. But, is that the best thing for him? He won't know a *mudder's* love."

"Jah, but he'd have a *vadder's* love."

"I'd like him to have both and be part of a family. Maybe that's the gift I can give him. The gift of letting him go. I guess that's just what Lucinda thinks she's doing."

"Lucinda doesn't want to be a *mudder."*

"It doesn't matter what her reasons. She can't be his parent for whatever reason, but she does want what's best and doesn't believe she's the best person to raise him."

Michaela nodded, but couldn't help feeling that Lucinda should've at least tried. Maybe she was thinking about herself more than the baby.

Mervin made arrangements to call for her the next day, and together they'd go back to the phone store.

CHAPTER 14

"THANKS FOR COMING and collecting me today," Michaela smiled at Mervin. "I knew Hannah would want to take her buggy because she's visiting the new twins again—Karen's twins. I haven't even met Karen. I wonder what it's like to have twins?"

"Double the work of having one, I'd say." He chuckled and she laughed.

"I think it would be lovely. Two babies instead of one; it would be so cute."

"I guess so," he said.

"You want twins?" She stared at him until he answered.

"I can't say I've ever thought too much about it."

"I have. I think it would be a blessing to have twins. Do you know what kind of phone you're going to buy?"

"I got instructions from Lucinda."

"I know, I was just thinking you might not know what you're doing." She giggled.

"I'm actually just getting the cheapest phone. Hopefully, no one will be able to trace it. She's going to destroy the phone after she makes contact with her brother."

"It's a waste."

"Not really. It's being safe."

"Okay. I just hope you know what you doing. I know Lucinda thinks the baby will have a better life, but what if she's wrong? No one loved me too much and I was passed around all over the place."

"Hmm. It would be a little different with the *boppli* being so young. You were older when your parents died."

"I guess that's true."

While keeping an eye on the road, Mervin looked into the trees by the side of the road as they passed, hoping she wouldn't say anything else. He was used to the quiet as he drove his buggy alone and found it relaxing. Michaela talking for the sake of hearing her own voice made him tense.

When they drove past the store, he tied up the buggy a little further along the road.

"Do you want me to come with you?" she asked.

"Sure, if you want to."

When they both walked in, a young man greeted

them and Mervin told him exactly what he wanted. They were out of there in less than fifteen minutes.

"I'm surprised how easy that was." Michaela stepped onto the sidewalk and glanced back at Mervin.

"Me too." At least she had stopped talking while they were in the store.

"Did you see everyone staring at us?"

"Were they?"

"A hush fell across the place as soon as we walked in and they were all looking."

He chuckled. "I didn't even notice."

"I did. Where are we going now?"

"We're going back to Lucinda to give her the phone. Unless there was somewhere you wanted to go?"

"Nee."

Mervin passed Michaela the phone to hold on the drive back to Lucinda. When they got onto the quieter roads, Michaela talked even more than she had on the way there.

"You don't say much."

He was thankful they were almost back at the old mill. "I only talk when I have something to say."

"Well, that must be almost never."

He didn't make a comment on that. And he was glad that she hadn't taken what he'd said in a bad way.

As they pulled up, Lucinda opened the door and looked nervously around. "Did you get it?" she called out.

"We did." Michaela jumped down from the buggy holding up the package and a smile spread across Lucinda's face and she stepped back into the building.

When they were all inside, Mervin took the wrapping off the phone.

Lucinda held out her hand. "It's the same unit as the one I asked for?"

"Yep, and he said it was ready to go."

She took it from him. "Please have some charge on it, please have some charge on it." She pressed a button and the phone made a tinkling sound. "Yes." She spun in a circle holding the phone up in the air. "Watch the baby for me. He'll wake in a minute and his bottle's on the table," she said to no one in particular as she walked outside pressing numbers into the phone.

"I just hope everything turns out well," Michaela said, pushing open the bedroom door. The baby was lying there asleep and Mervin looked over her shoulder. "He's just so beautiful. So peaceful. He doesn't know he has an uncertain future."

"Don't say that, Michaela."

She turned around and stared at Mervin. "It's true. Why shouldn't I say the truth?"

He took off his hat and held it against his chest. "I don't like to think about it. We have to help her find a home for the baby."

"We?"

He nodded. "I'd be happy for you to help me if you'd like to."

"I'd love to. We both want what's best for this little *bu.*"

"He's answered," Lucinda yelled from outside.

Michaela wasn't happy about that. The baby was just one step closer to losing his mother.

Mervin smiled "He's perfect."

"He is. I wish he was mine. I'd hate to see him upset —ever. He deserves such a good life."

"We'll see he gets it."

"You mean it?" She looked into Mervin's face, and he nodded.

When the baby started fussing, Michaela picked him up. "She said there's a bottle somewhere."

"On the table."

Mervin followed Michaela out of the room and soon they were huddled together on the small couch feeding the baby, while Lucinda paced up and down outside talking into the phone.

Michaela cradled the baby in her arms as he sucked on his bottle. Then she put her finger near his hand and he opened his eyes and then closed his fist tightly around her finger. "Oh, look, Mervin, he's clutching me. Now he's looking at me. Hello, little *boppli.*"

Then Lucinda burst into the building. "He's booked me a ticket over the Internet while I was talking to him."

Michaela looked up at her. "When for?"

"I'm to go to New York and from there I get the

flight the day after tomorrow. He's put money in my account to travel."

"Will you be okay going back to New York? What if you're recognized?" Mervin asked.

Before Lucinda answered, Michaela asked, "What about the *boppli?*"

Lucinda ignored Michaela and answered Mervin's question. "I'll have to take that risk if I'm to get out of the country."

"Are you taking the *boppli* with you?" Michaela asked.

"Nee." She shook her head. "Mervin, can you do me another favor?"

"What?"

"Come with me to a lawyer first thing tomorrow. I need to sign over the rights of my baby to you and then you can have the say-so of who adopts him. I'd do it, but obviously, I don't have the time now."

He gulped. "Me?"

"Jah. You're the only person who can do this because you're the only person I trust. I know you'll make a good decision. He really deserves the very best start in life."

That irritated Michaela. "Take him with you."

"Don't make me feel bad about this, Michaela. The world isn't as bright as you think. You'll understand when you're older. Mervin and I have lived a little longer. I want him to have a good life with an Amish family somewhere and when he's older he can make his own decision where he wants to live. Staying in the community wasn't right for me or my brother, but it wasn't a bad start. It'll keep him safe for as long as possible and maybe it'll be right for him."

"What's wrong with staying in the community?" Michaela asked.

Mervin put his hand up. "Michaela, this might not be the right time to talk about things like this."

Michaela pouted. "She's leaving tomorrow. This is the only time left."

Lucinda sat down beside Michaela, causing Michaela to have to move closer to Mervin to make room. "You're a sweet girl and it's kind of you to try to help, but the answer for my child is to be raised by somebody else and for him not to stay with me. Get it?"

"How do you know if you don't try? Why don't you stay in the community with him?"

Lucinda shook her head. "I'm not gonna stick around the Amish community and become a baby factory with some man telling me what to do and how to live my life, no sirree. I'm moving to England and starting a new life. Who knows, I might meet a European prince and become a queen."

"Won't you worry about him every day?"

"Not if Mervin finds him a good home. Will you do that for me, Mervin?"

Michaela was upset. The baby wasn't a puppy to hand over to someone else, and that's how she was treating him. What if Mervin didn't have good judgement over what family was going to be a good fit for the baby?

Mervin ran a hand through his hair. "Okay. If that's what you want and you're sure this is the only way."

"I am."

Lucinda took the baby from Michaela and hugged him.

Michaela wanted to keep him. She'd give him the best life she could, and she'd never abandon him or leave him to be cared for by a stranger. Then Lucinda handed the baby back to Michaela and walked to the other side of the room. All the while, Mervin sat next to Michaela in silence.

Then a loud crashing sound shuddered through Michaela, startling her and the baby. She looked up to see Lucinda hitting the cell phone with a hammer, crouching down on the stone floor. "What's she doing that for?"

"So it can't be traced," Mervin said.

Once Lucinda was finished, she stood up. "I should've ordered a taxi for tomorrow before I did that."

"I can take you somewhere," Michaela offered.

"No wait. I'm not thinking properly. Mervin, we've got to find a lawyer first thing tomorrow."

He nodded. "I'll take the day off work."

"Will you be right to look after the *boppli* from tomorrow?" Lucinda looked pleadingly at Mervin. "If not, I could put him in foster care."

"Nee," Michaela blurted out.

"I'll figure something out," Mervin said.

"I'll come tomorrow to help out."

Lucinda nodded. "That would be good if you could, Michaela. Once I'm in town, I'll catch the bus to New York and make my way to the airport."

CHAPTER 15

THE NEXT DAY, Michaela again told Hannah she had something important to do with Mervin. Hannah smirked as though it was a date, and Michaela didn't tell her otherwise.

After Mervin collected Michaela, they picked up the baby and Lucinda, and then headed into town. At their third lawyer's office—attempting to find a lawyer who would even talk with them without a prior appointment—Lucinda and Mervin were successful.

While Lucinda and Mervin were in the lawyer's office making the arrangements, Michaela sat in the waiting area with the grumbling baby. He was tired and now he was hungry. Michaela fished in Lucinda's bag and found the bottle and popped it into his mouth. He sucked on it eagerly and half closed his eyes.

Settling back into the chair, Michaela enjoyed the way it felt to hold him. Then she looked down at him again expecting to see him sleeping, but he was staring up into her face. She could feel the love passing between them. It was a heavenly moment.

"That's a beautiful baby you've got there."

Michaela looked up at the young woman sitting a few seats away. "Thank you. He is beautiful."

"How old?"

"Just three weeks."

"Oh, you forget how tiny they are at that age, don't you?"

"I don't know." Harmlessly playing make-believe that he was hers, she said, "I've only got the one. What about you? Do you have any children?"

"Yes, I have two boys. They're five and six, both in school now."

"Such lovely ages."

"My advice is to enjoy every age. I spent too long hoping they'd grow up, and now they're in school and I wish they were still home with me. Enjoy every stage they're at."

Michaela stared at her in wide-eyed amusement. She hadn't asked for any child-rearing tips. "Thank you. I will."

At that moment, both Lucinda and Mervin walked back into the reception area. Michaela stood and smiled at the young woman. "Nice talking to you."

"And you."

Then Michaela joined her friends as they pushed

open the glass office door onto the sidewalk. "What happened?" she whispered to Mervin.

"I'll tell you later."

Michaela noticed they both seemed stressed and unhappy, so she didn't ask anything further. It couldn't have been easy for Lucinda to sign the rights of her baby over to another person, even though this was what she'd said she wanted.

Suddenly, Lucinda whistled for a taxi and raised her arm in the air to flag it down. When the taxi stopped, she opened the back door and then hugged Mervin goodbye, did her best to hug Michaela, who was still holding the baby, and then kissed her son.

"Wait! Your bag's in the buggy," Michaela said.

"That's all for the baby. I'm just going in what I've got on."

Then Michaela recalled that she'd worn the same thing all the time; the ripped jeans, the cream sweater pulled over the blue t-shirt. She'd escaped in those clothes and had no others.

"Hold him before you go, just one last time." Michaela moved the baby slightly toward Lucinda.

"No. I must go."

"Contact me when you arrive, let me know you're okay," Mervin said as she got into the taxi.

"I will." When Lucinda had strapped on her seat belt, she lowered the window. "Find him a home, Mervin."

"I'll help him," Michaela called out before Mervin had a chance to answer.

"Thank you, Michaela."

"We definitely will," was the last thing Mervin said before the taxi pulled away from the curb.

Side-by-side, they stood and watched the baby's mother leave. Tears came to Michaela's eyes and she couldn't stop them.

Mervin glanced at her, and then did a double take, staring at her. "What's the matter?"

"I feel the baby's pain. I can't believe that she's gone just like that. This little *boppli* is alone and deserted."

"Nee, he's not. He has the both of us."

"Jah, but how can we know that in a few years he won't cry himself to sleep because he feels alone and unloved." She stared down at the sleeping baby in her arms. "I can't allow him to ever feel that pain."

Mervin saw that he'd just gotten a glimpse of the real Michaela. She'd known that pain of being alone. The bold front she put on wasn't the person she was deep down inside. She put layers of boldness around herself to protect a soft center, he figured. "For certain, Michaela, we won't let him down. We'll never let him feel that pain."

Through teary eyes, she asked, "Do you mean it?"

He put his arm loosely around Michaela's shoulder. "We have to trust in *Gott* that He has His hands on this little *bu."*

"Who are we kidding, Mervin? We both know what

it's like to be without parents and it's not good. We have to find the very best parents for him so he never knows what it's like to have that hollow feeling in the pit of your stomach." She shook her head and puffed out her rosy cheeks.

Mervin looked down into Michaela's teary blue-gray eyes, and wanted to heal her pain every bit as much as he wanted to look after the baby. "Then, we'll find a way to do it."

"Are you sure?"

"Very sure."

She rested her head on his arm as they stayed by the side of the road. After a moment, he looked up in the direction the taxi had gone. "I hope Lucinda makes it."

"What do you mean?"

"That criminal might have people watching the airports. I've asked her to call me from a payphone when she arrives safely in London."

"Will she call your phone in the barn?"

"Nee, the lumberyard. I gave her that number. There's always someone handy to answer the phone."

"And if she doesn't?"

"I'll have to call the police."

She hugged the baby to herself. "I hope it doesn't come to that. What will we do with him now, Mervin? Right now, and where will he sleep tonight? We can't hide him forever."

"I have no idea. We've got a few hours to come up with a plan."

"Well, you've been given the power to make the decision. You'll have to look for families who need another child. Perhaps there's some childless couple out there somewhere. I don't know. I guess you'd like him to stay close." When she noticed his white face, she knew something wasn't quite right. "Are you okay?"

He took a deep breath. "Let's stop somewhere for a bite to eat and we can figure this whole thing out."

Mervin sat in the booth in the diner, staring down at the baby who was now cradled in his arms, and Michaela knew he was having a hard time with what had to come next. The baby's future rested on Mervin's shoulders.

On the table in front of them were the fries and burgers they'd ordered, but neither of them was hungry.

"I don't want to see the little guy go to just anyone. I feel like he's mine. I was in the next room when he was born. I held him minutes after, even before Lucinda did."

"He is yours, Mervin. Officially, you're in charge of him now."

He shook his head. "Not really. What we didn't tell you is that the lawyer we saw couldn't help us and there was no time to find another lawyer who could find a loophole."

"What?"

"The thing is, he has no birth certificate and Lucinda only had her passport and they wanted more ID if they were to help us."

"Ach nee! That's awful. That's not good enough. She should've thought about this before. Why didn't you say something to her at the time?"

"She couldn't help it. Anyway, with no official record of his birth there was nothing the lawyer could do. We had no time to go looking for another lawyer, or get the proper paperwork in order."

Michaela leaned forward. "What you're saying is, the authorities could come and take him away and you'd have no way to stop them?"

He nodded. *"Jah."*

"Mervin, we can't let that happen."

"I know." He breathed out heavily. "We have to think of something."

Too upset to eat, Michaela sipped her soda through the straw hoping the sugar would at least give her some much-needed energy. "Let's keep him."

"How? You live in Wiseman's Grove and I live here with my *grossmammi."*

She gulped. He didn't take a hint too well. Marriage was their best answer. "I could move here."

"And?"

"We could marry, and then no one would take him away. I'd do it if you'd be willing."

"Hmm. Is this another joke?"

"Not this time."

He looked deep in thought as he stared at the fries that were getting cold. "Could you marry me without being in love with me?"

She had hoped he was starting to like her. "I've never really expected love in my life after my parents died. I'm not saying that to feel sorry for myself or to make you feel sorry for me. That's just the way it's always been. We could be a good team, a good duo, a good unit."

He laughed. "You're mad."

"Am I? You said you wanted a large family, didn't you?"

"*Jah,* but in my head, it played out differently."

"I want a family." She shook her head. "Anyway, it was just a thought. At least I had one. Now it's your turn to put forward an idea."

He looked down at the sleeping baby, and then looked across at Michaela. "Even if we went back today and announced we're getting married, how would we explain this little guy?"

Michaela thought fast. "We're in love and you met someone who couldn't keep him and they've agreed to a private adoption. Someone you met on the outside."

"Hmm."

"Oh, Mervin, they'll think he's yours, won't they?"

He breathed out heavily. "Maybe. I hadn't even

thought of that. But I'll say he's not and they'll have to believe me. The bishop's a decent man."

"Jah, and he'll expect you to tell him the truth and you won't be. Rebecca will know the truth."

"Rebecca only knows Lucinda was the mother, and that she was in danger from the father of the *boppli.* She'll keep quiet; she said it's part of her vocation. How about I have him at night, and you have him while I'm at work?"

"You have to work. Why don't I have him at night and you can see him in the afternoon? I've got that big bedroom all to myself and it doesn't matter if I'm tired through the day. I'll still be able to help Hannah out while I have him close by."

He slowly nodded.

She wanted him to be more enthusiastic about the idea. In him, she saw a decent, kind and caring man just like she'd always dreamed of marrying. Why wasn't he having similar thoughts? "Forget it. There must be another way." She'd much prefer if he was showing some excitement about the prospect.

He struggled to tear off a piece of hamburger.

"I'll hold him while you eat," she offered.

"Nee, I can manage."

It touched her that he was so fond of the baby.

Once he'd eaten a little, he said, "I thought it would be easier than this. How can I find a home for him when I have no official documentation? As soon as anyone finds that out, he'll be taken away from me for sure."

She nodded. "The fewer people who know about that, the better."

"The boy needs a good start in life and I haven't met a woman I've fallen madly in love with and I doubt I'll ever have those feelings. Were you serious about us marrying? You joked about it the other day. Are you certain it wasn't a joke again today?"

"Nee, I already told you I was being serious just now."

"That could be the best solution, if you'd be willing. Could you see yourself being married to a man like me? I've not got much to offer except my share of the lumberyard and the old family home behind it."

"A share in a lumberyard and a *haus?"*

"Jah."

"What's wrong with that?" she asked.

"Nothing. I'm telling you what I've got. You should know that if we're going to tie the knot."

She giggled, more at his silly grin than what he'd just said. Then she got serious. "I have nothing and I mean it. Not like your kind of nothing. I've got zero, zilch, nada. I only own what I have in the bedroom at the Shroders. And, I don't even know how long I'll be there or even if I'm meant to go back to Vera's place." She huffed.

"A person is not defined by their possessions or

where they live. What matters are the intentions of the heart."

She stared into his hazel eyes and in that moment, felt herself fall a little bit in love with him.

"Together, we'll have all we need." Then he looked down at the baby. "Look at him."

Assuming they'd decided they would marry, the practical side of her kicked in. "The first thing we'll have to do is give him a name. I've always like Ezekiel, that is if you don't have a preference."

"Hmm, Ezekiel is a bit old sounding to me."

"Call him after you. Mervin."

He shook his head. "I wouldn't do that to him."

"Ethan?"

He shrugged his shoulders. "That's okay."

"It's got to be more than just okay. What about Abner?"

Mervin smiled and shrugged his shoulders once more.

"Okay... Well, his mother's name's Lucinda, so what about Luke? Luke Mervin Breuer. Then he'd have your name as his middle name."

"That's nice. He'll have something of his mother too, and she did suggest we call him Mervin. Hmm, I think Lucinda would be agreeable to that."

Michaela nodded. "Now, what's the plan?"

"Keeping him is the only way to know he'll be raised safe and within our community and not end up somewhere he's not loved."

"Agreed."

"I worry about you though, Michaela. It's not fair to you to marry me just for the sake of Luke. A few weeks ago, you didn't even know me. You could've had a whole different future."

"This is the future I choose." She hoped one day he'd fall in love with her because the more they spent time with each other, the more she liked him.

"I need time to think this through."

She shook her head. "There's not much time left. I'm expected home and if we have to tell Elspeth and the bishop and Hannah a story tonight, we'll have to think of it now and tell them in the next few hours. Luke has to sleep somewhere tonight."

He sighed. "You're right. Just give me a couple of minutes without speaking." Staring at her with pleading eyes, he added, "Just two minutes? Can you manage that?"

"Okay. Shall I take Luke?"

He nodded and she walked to his side of the table, picked him up and he started crying. She leaned down, and whispered in Mervin's ear, "He knows you're his *vadder* already and doesn't want to leave." She gave a little giggle, straightened up, and then held the baby against her shoulder. "I'll walk outside with him. Let me know when you've finished your thinking."

"Denke, I will."

She turned back, and said, "I'll just say this before I go."

He shook his head and sighed. "I knew you wouldn't be able to keep quiet."

Ignoring him, she said, "When I arrived in this beautiful place, I had a feeling in the pit of my stomach that this would be my 'forever home.' In the past, I told myself I'd have to wait until I got to my heavenly home to feel comfortable. Perhaps I was wrong about that part." Michaela carefully pulled the soft cotton wrap higher over the baby's head, and then made her way outside.

Mervin watched the young woman walk away with Luke. Marrying Michaela was the best way for him to keep the baby, but could he do that to himself? Sure, she was beautiful, but she drove him crazy with her incessant chatter. His quiet life would be a thing of the past. On the flip side, she was a decent and kind-hearted person and they held the same views on family and loyalty.

Then he explored the possibility of losing control of Luke's welfare. Lucinda had done an injustice leaving as quickly as she had without doing more to secure Luke's future. She'd heaped a burden onto his shoulders, by leaving so quickly. He couldn't stand by and refuse to help.

He looked out the window at Michaela as she paced up and down, her mouth moving, no doubt, saying soft words to the baby. Then it hit him. He would be giving Michaela a home as much as he would the baby. From what she'd told him, she had no place she could call home. Was it a coincidence that *Gott* had placed before him this woman and this child? He was the key to giving both of them a future, and by doing that, his reward would be something he'd always wanted—to be a father.

CHAPTER 16

MICHAELA WALKED BACK and forth outside the diner praying to God that His perfect will would be done. If she'd been a normal girl with a normal life, she might not be so keen for this to work out.

But she'd never had a life like other Amish girls. Back when her parents had been alive they'd fought and bickered behind closed doors, and presented something far different to the community, who saw them as the perfect family.

Having a pleasant home environment was something dear to Michaela's heart. To wake up in a house bathed in tranquillity rather than feeling the prickles of tension waiting for one of her parents to explode over the smallest of things. Yet, when they both died within months of each other, she was left alone. Having fighting parents was much better than having no parents at all, she soon found out. Her history had caused her to decide that things would be different if she were ever blessed with a family. Her children would have the security of a quiet and happy home.

As she lulled the baby back to sleep, she looked through the window of the diner and caught Mervin's eye and they exchanged smiles.

If God willed it, Mervin would agree to marry her and together they'd raise Luke as their own. It made sense that this was His plan. Was Mervin her answer to happiness?

When she glanced at him again, he beckoned for her to come inside. With the baby in her arms, she hurried back and sat down in front of him. From the smile on his face, she knew the answer was the one she'd hoped for.

"OKAY, how are we going to do this?" he asked.

She licked her lips. "What have you decided?"

"If you're willing … and you're absolutely sure, I'd love to marry you."

She looked into his hazel eyes and was pleased he'd used the word, love. "If you're sure, then let's do it." Was wanting him to love her a further sign that she was falling in love with him?

He chuckled and she joined in with a giggle. It was unbelievable that she was marrying someone with scarcely knowing him, but she knew the bishop and his wife thought highly of him and that spoke volumes.

"How do we go about it? We'll have to say something about Luke and where he came from, and why… Why are we getting married so fast?"

Mervin raised his eyebrows. "Oh, we are?"

Michaela nodded. "We should marry as soon as we can since we have Luke to care for."

He said, "That's right. I guess. We tell the bishop we've fallen madly in love, we're getting married as soon as he will allow and we're adopting Luke."

"He won't buy it. Not the part about falling in love, and he won't buy the Luke part."

"Okay... Why don't we tell him the truth?"

Michaela gasped. "What?"

He chuckled. "Remember the truth?"

"But … but … you don't want anyone to know about …"

"That's all I can think of. I don't think we've got any choice. If we tell Bishop Elmer the truth, he can help us protect Luke. It'll all be easier when we're married. Nobody else needs to know except for the bishop."

"And Hannah."

"I guess." He nodded. "Let's do this. We'll talk with him and then we'll tell Elspeth what's happening."

"Will we tell her the truth too?" Michaela asked.

"*Nee,* I don't think we can."

"Oh." Michaela hoped old Elspeth wouldn't have a heart attack when they told her they were getting married. She'd only met her once.

"We'll pretend we're in love and that's the reason we're marrying, that's the best way."

Michaela nodded. "Where will we live?"

"With my *grossmammi.* She's got spare rooms."

"You said you had a *haus?"*

"I've got people living in it right now. We could move in when they move out, but *Mammi's* more comfortable in her own home. She'll always live with us. I guess it makes sense to keep living in her *haus."*

Michaela nodded. "Suits me. I don't mind where we live."

He leaned forward. "This is your last chance to back out."

She smiled at him. "I won't. I've always wanted my own family. I'm happy to marry you and care for Luke. I'll look after him as though he was my own. He will be my own. Our own."

"I'm happy to hear it. This is our answer. Let's go."

To THE BUZZ of Michaela's planning, and expressing her hopes that Elspeth wouldn't mind sharing her house with another woman, they traveled to Bishop Elmer's *haus.*

When the buggy came to a halt, Michaela was overwhelmed. "I hope he takes it well."

"Of course he will. He'll be pleased. He encourages people to marry."

"I know, but we'll have to tell him everything about Luke and Lucinda. Don't leave anything out."

"If I do, I'm sure you'll remind me."

She nodded. "That's right. I will."

WHEN HANNAH OPENED the door and saw the baby, every question under the sun was thrown at them. Then the younger boys gathered around to get a look at the baby. Mervin did his best to avoid answering, saying he'd wait until he talked with Bishop Elmer.

Michaela got to the point. "Mrs. Shroder, we both need to see Bishop Elmer as a matter of urgency."

Hannah immediately sent the boys to their rooms. They weren't happy about that, going by their faces, but they did what they were told. Once all the boys were gone, she asked Michaela. "You need to see Elmer about the *boppli?*"

"Jah," Michaela and Mervin said together.

Two minutes later, they were both sitting in front of the bishop with Luke fast asleep in Michaela's arms.

Mervin told the bishop all that had happened with Lucinda and how he came to have the baby, and then ended the story with another piece of information. "Michaela has agreed to marry me."

The bishop didn't seem particularly overjoyed at that bit of news. Twitching movements of his lips caused his long graying beard to move about as he looked at Michaela. "Is that right?"

"Jah."

"Is this marriage just for the sake of the *boppli?* Because marriage is something that should be thought about long and hard before two people make that decision."

"We're aware of that. And, Michaela's the only woman for me."

"And I feel the same about Mervin. He's the only one for me—and we're adopting Luke." She gave Mervin a look because he'd forgotten to mention that part.

"That's right, we are."

The bishop adjusted his thin-rimmed glasses. "This is rather sudden, don't you think? You've been here for what, Michaela? Is it three weeks?"

"A little longer. *Jah,* and we know it's sudden, but that's ..."

Mervin interrupted. "It is fast and we've talked about it. Neither of us has felt this way before."

"And, how old are you, Michaela?"

"Nearly nineteen."

"I see. I can't stop the both of you, but I do recommend you wait."

"We thought you'd say that. How long would you say we should wait?"

The bishop chuckled. "I can remember what it was like to be young and in love. I can't put you through the burden of waiting a long time until you can be man and wife and start your lives together."

"So, we can?" Michaela asked.

"You can. If anyone asks, and I'm sure they will, I'll tell everyone Luke is a foundling and you've taken steps to give him a home. That's the truth and there's no need for anyone to know more than that."

Mervin nodded. *"Denke,* and I'll do my best to get in contact with Lucinda and get the proper documentation to make the adoption official."

Michaela nodded in agreement as well, but didn't even know if Mervin had Lucinda's brother's address.

"If I can borrow Michaela some more I'd like to deliver the news of my future new bride to my *grossmammi* tonight. Then I'll have her back here at a reasonable hour."

The bishop nodded. "I'll have Hannah keep your meal hot, Michaela."

"Denke. I don't think I'll be late." She looked at Mervin. "Will I?"

"Nee."

When they walked out of the living room, Hannah was waiting and the boys weren't anywhere to be seen.

"Hannah, these two are getting married very soon and adopting this *boppli."*

Hannah opened her mouth in shock, and closed it, and then said, "That is good news. Congratulations to the both of you."

"Denke," they both said.

"Where did he come from?" Hannah stepped forward to look at Luke.

"His name's Luke," Michaela told her not knowing what else to say.

"I'll tell you soon," the bishop told Hannah. "These two need to tell Elspeth the news and the *boppli* will be staying here until their wedding."

"Jah, jah of course. Another wedding. We'll have it here, will we?"

It was clear Hannah was excited about news of a wedding.

"I don't know." Now Michaela felt overwhelmed.

The bishop put his arm around his wife's shoulder. "There's plenty of time to think about that."

Hannah nodded. "Will they marry before Deborah and William Bronstein?"

The bishop nodded. *"Jah,* they will."

Hannah said to the young couple, "You do what you have to do. While you're gone, I'll set up a crib. It's not long since we put Andrew's in the attic. We'll clean it up ready for Luke and have it ready in your room?"

"Jah. Denke, Hannah, and I'll be home as soon as I can."

CHAPTER 17

AS THEY TRAVELED to Elspeth's house, Michaela wondered about Mervin's day-to-day life. "You don't seem to be looking after Elspeth very much."

He glanced at her. "I come home during the day, on my break, and cut the vegetables for dinner. And on the weekends, I make casseroles to freeze on days when I'm not able to get home. I normally do all the cooking… well, most of it. And on Saturday afternoon, I do any cleaning she can't do."

"Oh, I see. You haven't been there all day today." Elspeth had even said that he was gone all day. She'd said nothing about him coming home in the middle of his work day.

"Don't worry, she's good enough. She can look after herself to a degree."

She felt silly about her comment, and for doubting him. "I didn't mean to upset you."

"You didn't."

"I'm nervous. What do you think she'll say about the *boppli?*

He shrugged his shoulders. "I think she'll have more to say about us getting married."

"Oh no." She bit down on to the inside of her lip. "This is making me scared."

"Don't worry, it'll be much easier than talking to the bishop. I can tell you that much."

"Will it?"

"Much easier. He grilled us."

"I think … he didn't really, I mean he just let us do our thing anyway in the end. He just let us do what we wanted." She yawned and quickly covered her mouth.

"Am I keeping you awake?"

"Jah." She giggled. "I haven't been able to sleep much since I met you."

He laughed. "Is that true, or is it just since you found out about Lucinda and Luke?"

"Yes, that's probably it. Once I found out your secret, it became mine, too. And I'm not that comfortable with keeping secrets."

"Me neither, but you gotta do what you gotta do in these situations."

"I guess so." She looked down at the baby in her arms, and then lowered her head to give him a quick kiss on his bald head. "I can't believe he's going to be mine. I hope nothing goes wrong with our plans."

"Relax, I don't think anything can go wrong now. The only thing might be if Lucinda changes her mind."

"That would be a good thing. It wouldn't be a bad thing because he's rightfully hers."

"I'm sure everything will be fine. She was pretty firm about him having one future and her having another very different one."

When they stopped at Mervin and Elspeth's house it was well and truly night time. They saw the door open and Elspeth's silhouette appeared in the doorway.

"She's been waiting for you."

"Just take my lead and don't say too much."

"Good. I won't say anything."

He got out of the buggy, secured it, and then helped Michaela out with Luke.

When they got closer, Elspeth greeted them and then stared at the baby. "Who's this little fella?"

"Come back inside and sit down, *Mammi.* We've got a lot to tell you."

"Oh, Mervin, he's not yours, is he?"

He laughed. *"Nee,* well, he's not mine yet. I'm not the *vadder."*

Once they were seated in the living room opposite *Mammi,* who sat in her usual armchair, Mervin said, "I have asked Michaela to marry me and she has agreed."

"I'm happy for you both. Where does the *boppli* fit into everything? Whose is he?"

Michaela had to speak because Mervin just sat

there. "He has no parents and we're going to adopt him."

"Where did you find him?"

Michaela saw Mervin's face grow white.

He opened his mouth but had trouble getting the words out quick enough. "I knew someone—"

Even though he'd asked her to keep quiet, she had to help him again. "What Mervin means is he knew someone, who was just a friend, and she couldn't keep the baby. It was very sad and then when we found out that we were in love, Mervin stopped the woman giving the baby up for adoption. We offered to adopt him and the mother agreed. We've spoken to the bishop and he's given us the okay. He's getting back to us with a wedding date. We're getting married as soon as possible."

"I see." Elspeth turned to Mervin. "Why didn't you just say so? This is *wunderbaar* news." She turned back to Michaela. "Welcome to the family, Michaela. Will you stay for dinner?"

"No, maybe another night? The bishop and Hannah are arranging a crib to be put in my room for him."

Elspeth's eyes fell to the baby. "Might I hold him?"

"*Jah*, of course." Michaela stood and then placed the baby in *Mammi's* arms.

She looked adoringly at the baby, and then looked up at Mervin. "Where will you live?"

"We were hoping we might all be able to live here with you."

The old woman's face lit up. "That would be *wunderbaar,* if you don't mind sharing the house with an old lady, Michaela."

Michaela giggled. "Well, if you don't mind having me here, I'll be very happy to be here. He's a good *bu,* he won't bother you because he hardly makes any noise. He rarely cries except when he's a little bit tired and it's not long before he goes to sleep. He won't be any trouble."

"Trouble or not, this makes me very happy. I've been so worried about Mervin for so long."

"That's enough about me, *denke, Mammi."*

"You've come along when he needed you, Michaela. You saved him from having a lonely life when I go to *Gott."*

Mervin shook his head. "Well, I'll take you back now, Michaela."

"Would you like to come for the ride, Elspeth?"

She chortled. "You can call me *Mammi,* and *nee,* I'm sure you two have plenty of private things to talk about between yourselves. I've heated the soup you made, Mervin. I'll keep your dinner warm for you. Unless you're eating at Hannah's *haus?"*

"I'll come back here. *Denke, Mammi."*

Once Michaela had Luke in her arms once more, Mervin quickly ushered her out of the house and into the buggy.

"That went very well. She doesn't even mind me living in the *haus."*

"There's plenty of space." He collected the reins and clicked his horse forward.

"I can't believe this is all happening so fast. Before I came here, I had nothing and now I have you, I have *Mammi* and Luke. How quickly *Gott* works His miracles."

He chuckled. "I've never had anyone call me a miracle before."

"You are. You're part of my miracle."

CHAPTER 18

THAT NIGHT, Michaela stared in disbelief at the baby in the crib next to her bed. While she'd been gone, Hannah had carefully set aside a stack of clean diapers in the room, and had greeted her with the news she'd prepared two bottles and they were waiting in the gas-powered fridge. But, she couldn't allow herself to relax and enjoy what was happening just in case it all fell apart. No, she wouldn't relax until she and Mervin were married. Then it would all be real.

WORD of the wedding had spread like fire over parched grass, and the very next day a whole bunch of women were in Hannah's house fussing over Michaela. Plans were being made for the wedding and they were deciding between themselves who was to do each task.

There was the menu of the wedding breakfast to decide, the cakes to bake, Michaela's wedding dress to sew, Mervin's suit to tailor, and all the outfits of the special wedding attendants. All manner of decisions were being made with Michaela scarcely opening her mouth.

When the women finally left, Michaela and Hannah were exhausted. "*Denke* for doing all this, Hannah. Can I call you Hannah rather than Mrs. Shroder? I always call you Hannah in my mind."

Hannah slumped into a kitchen chair beside her. "Sure that's fine, and you're very welcome."

"It's amazing how quickly things can be organized."

"That's one thing we're good at doing around here."

"I noticed."

Hannah leaned forward. "You'll be a good *mudder* for Luke."

"*Denke*. That makes me feel better. It's such a burden keeping a secret sometimes, so I'm glad you know all of it. I'll do my best to be the best parent ever."

"We have to hope and pray nobody comes looking for Lucinda." Hannah shook her head. "She always was a different kind of a girl, never content with what she had. I always thought she'd be one to leave the community."

"I guess that people, some people, just want different things sometimes."

"That's true enough. Well, we've got a few weeks until the wedding." Hannah glanced at the clock. "And I don't have a lot of time before the boys come home. Do you want to write letters to tell your friends? We could both write letters together. I'll get us notepaper and envelopes."

"I don't have many friends because I've been … I've lived in so many different communities."

"Surely you've got a lot of friends in Wiseman's Valley?"

Michaela giggled. "It's Wiseman's Grove."

"So it is." Hannah laughed. "I don't know why I said that. I've written to Vera a few times over the years and I know very well where she lives."

"Maybe she never got some of your letters."

"That's true. And now we know why."

Both of them laughed.

ONCE THEY WERE SETTLED back at the kitchen table and ready to write, Michaela poised her pen over the paper. "I'll write to Vera and she can tell the others. I'm blessed that everybody's doing so much for the wedding and they hardly know me."

"We know you. You're one of *Gott's* children. That's all we need to know. And you're marrying Mervin, a man many of us thought would never marry."

That was news to Michaela. "I can't imagine why, he's so nice. Is there anything bad I don't know about him?"

"Oh no. He's fine, nothing's wrong with him. I can't

imagine why he hasn't married before now. Perhaps he was just waiting for the right girl, and now here you are."

"That's right, here I am," Michaela said. Right at that moment they heard Luke's cries. "I better change his diaper, and give him his bottle."

"I'll heat it up for you."

"Denke, Hannah." Michaela walked into her bedroom hoping that nothing would stop the wedding from going ahead. She'd often felt that she wasn't important and she'd been placed on this earth to be one of the crowd. Now things had taken a turn. Today, people had fussed over her and asked her opinions on things as though she mattered. That was something that she didn't want to end.

WITH THEIR WEDDING WEEKS AWAY, Mervin and Michaela developed a routine. Mervin went directly to the bishop's house after work to collect Luke and Michaela. They would then spend the evening at Mervin's house until it was late, then he'd take them back again. Michaela got to know Elspeth better, and she helped around the house and cooked, leaving Mervin to spend time with Luke.

Elspeth had set up a bedroom for Michaela,, so Michaela and Luke could stay over on Friday and

Saturday nights. That way, Mervin got more time to spend with them.

Michaela saw a bright future for all, but in her heart, she expected things to go wrong at any moment. After all, things never had turned out well for her.

CHAPTER 19

A MONTH after sharing their news with the bishop, Michaela woke up. It was her wedding day. No one had come to take Luke away from them, and no criminals had come looking for Lucinda. Now all that could go wrong was if Mervin would change his mind, or Lucinda would arrive to reclaim Luke. She shrugged off her negativity and sat up and looked over at Luke. He was lying there in his crib, awake and looking around.

Michaela got out of bed. "Hello, little one."

His small mouth opened and then turned down at the corners, and he started to whimper. "Wait there. I'll get your bottle. *Mamm* just needs to change so I can get your bottle. I can't go into the Shroders' kitchen like this, can I?" That was the first time she'd called herself *Mamm* when she'd talked to him. She liked the way it felt and couldn't wait until he was old enough to call her *Mamm.* She exchanged her nightgown for a dress and slipped a band around her hair and swept it under her *kapp.*

She picked him up and took him inside the house. When she got to the kitchen, everyone was awake, eating, and they exchanged their good morning greetings.

Hannah said, "I was just about to get you and then I heard Luke cry. I've got his bottle warming up."

"Denke, Hannah." She yawned. "Am I running late? I didn't even look at the time."

"We need an early start. In a few minutes, the wagon with the benches will be here."

It was a huge undertaking to host a wedding. With the Shroder house being small, despite the Shroder's having had thirteen children, an extra annex was already set up outside to cope with all the cooking and food preparation. Much like the Sunday meetings, the furniture would be moved out of the house and all the church benches would be set up. Then the yard would be littered with tables and chairs. Like at most of the weddings, the food was help-yourself for the guests except for those at the main wedding table.

There was so much to be done. Michaela paced up and down the room, but Luke didn't stop crying and she didn't want him to upset the Shroder boys. "I'll change his diaper." She headed back to her room.

"I'll bring his bottle in to you."

"Denke, Hannah."

Michaela changed Luke's diaper, then Wendy arrived with her little sister, Cheryl Lee, and Wendy took the baby out of her hands.

"Gut mayrie."

"Morning, Wendy."

"It's your special day. I came early to help you."

"You could give him his bottle while I have a quick shower."

"Sure."

Michaela showered in double quick time and she came back to see Wendy sitting on her bed cuddling Luke, with Cheryl Lee close beside her helping to hold the baby's bottle.

"Denke for the help. I've got butterflies in my tummy already." While Michaela slipped on her mid-blue wedding dress, all she could hear was Wendy talking about Aedan.

"Has he said anything about me? Does he ask about me?"

Then Abigail walking in with Ferris interrupted them. "Ferris wanted to see the baby." She said hello to the two Byler girls and then looked at Michaela. "How are you doing, Michaela?"

"Great."

"You'll be married in a few hours and it'll be the start of a new life. Is Vera coming from …"

Michaela shook her head. *"Nee."*

Hannah put her head through the doorway. "Did someone say Vera's name?"

"Jah, I did," said Abigail.

Hannah walked in and passed Michaela a letter. "She's upset she can't come and she said to give you this letter on your wedding day."

Michaela took it from her and the chatter of the girls faded into the background as she read it. Vera had written that she wasn't well and that was why she'd sent her to Hannah's place. She went on to say how pleased she was that Michaela was getting married because she'd finally have a home of her own. Michaela looked up at Hannah. "Did you know she was ill?"

"Nee. She only told me in the letter she sent to me at the same time as the one she sent for you."

"I wonder why she never said anything. Do you know what is the matter with her?"

Hannah shook her head. "I know as much as you."

Michaela folded the letter away, placing it at the top of her suitcase. It felt better to learn there was a reason she'd been sent away. It wasn't because she was a nuisance. She hoped the illness wasn't serious, but feared it was.

Now Luke was no longer drinking, and Hannah scooped the baby up from Wendy. "I'll look after him for the day."

"I'll help too," said Abigail.

"You concentrate on everything else," Hannah told Michaela.

"Jah, and try to remember all you can about the day, and enjoy yourself," Abigail added.

Michaela gave a little giggle. "I will, Abigail."

Abigail grabbed hold of Ferris's hand and walked out the door with Hannah, who was holding Luke. Then, Cheryl Lee ran her hands up and down Michaela's wedding dress.

"Stop it, Cheryl Lee," her sister said.

"I'm just touching it."

"Michaela doesn't want your dirty paws all over it."

Cheryl Lee looked down at her hands. "They're clean."

Wendy rolled her eyes at her sister. "Sorry about her. *Mamm* said I couldn't come early unless I brought her too."

"Don't be sorry. You're blessed to have a *schweschder.*"

"Humph. You don't know her like I do."

"It doesn't matter. Nothing can replace family."

Wendy shook her head and Cheryl Lee promptly poked out her tongue at Wendy, causing Wendy to gasp. "See what she just did? She does stuff like that all the time."

"You'll appreciate her when you both get older."

"I'll have to wait and see, I guess."

Wendy bounded to her feet. "You haven't said anything about my dress." She spun around in a circle.

"It looks so pretty. I noticed it when you came in. That shade of blue suits you. It really lights up your eyes."

She sat back down on the bed. "I hope Aedan likes it."

"He won't even notice it, or you." Cheryl Lee folded her arms and glared at her sister.

"I'm going to marry him no matter what you think."

"And what about you, Cheryl Lee?" Michaela asked. "Is there anyone you like?"

Wendy got in first, and said, "She wouldn't tell you even if there was. She's sneaky."

Cheryl Lee giggled. "I am not."

"You are too."

When the girls heard rattling sounds they all rushed to the window. It was the wagon bringing the benches and the trestle tables. For the first time, nerves gnawed at Michaela's stomach instead of just feeling like butterflies. She was marrying someone who was little more than a stranger. A little over two months ago, she'd never heard of Mervin Breuer.

It was too late to back out now that all the preparations were done. Besides that, who would look after Luke? There was no choice but to go through with it. As she watched out the window, more people arrived. It was the women who'd come to help with the food preparations. The rest of the wedding guests weren't due to arrive for a couple more hours.

MICHAELA HOPED she looked good for her new husband. She wanted her marriage to be perfect and for her husband to adore her. More than anything, she wanted no arguments within the marriage like those she'd witnessed all too often between her parents. So opposed was she to couples arguing she was even prepared to agree with everything Mervin wanted just so there would be no cross words.

"Where will the ceremony be?" Wendy asked.

"In the *haus*."

"You must be nervous."

"How can you tell?"

"You've not said much."

Michaela nodded.

HALF AN HOUR LATER, Hannah knocked on the door and then opened it. "Plans have changed. The wedding will be in the yard. There are too many people here to have it in the *haus*. I didn't know we'd get this many."

"But all the benches are inside, aren't they?"

"The men are carrying them out now. I'll be back in ten minutes and then you'll have to come out. We'll be ready for you"

"Okay." Wendy and Michaela looked out the window. "I still haven't seen Mervin today."

Wendy dug her in the ribs. "There he is. He looks handsome in his dark suit."

Michaela scanned the crowd where Wendy was pointing and saw Mervin. He had on a wide brimmed black hat keeping his unruly hair in check, and a dark suit that fitted so well. Then the room swam and she lowered herself to the floor. Next thing she knew, she opened her eyes and saw Hannah and Abigail peering down at her.

Then Rebecca pushed everyone aside. "Are you okay, Michaela?"

"I fainted? I must've fainted." She saw she was on the floor and tried to sit up, but Rebecca told her to stay put.

"Has this happened before?" Rebecca asked.

"Nee, never. There was no reason for that to happen."

"Did you stand up suddenly?"

"We did. We were sitting on the bed and then we rushed to the window."

"It's probably just nerves. Are you nervous?" Rebecca asked.

"Jah, she would be," Hannah said.

"Wendy, get her some water, would you?"

They helped her sit up.

"I'll be okay in a minute. How long was I out of it?" Michaela asked.

"Only a minute at most," Hannah told her.

Wendy rushed back into the room and handed Michaela a glass of water, and she took a couple of large mouthfuls.

Abigail asked, "Will I tell them to delay things? They're waiting for us."

"Nee! I'll be okay."

"Surely they can wait a little longer," Rebecca said.

"I'll have a word with Elmer, letting him know that you're not feeling well and you need to sit. Otherwise you'll be standing for a good half hour. You'll have to stand for the important part."

"I can do that. *Denke,* Hannah."

Hannah headed out of the room to speak with the bishop.

Cheryl Lee who'd been quiet up until now, asked, "You're not pregnant, are you?"

Wendy gasped. "Cheryl Lee, get out of this room now! I'm going to tell *Mamm* what you just said."

Michaela found what she'd said funny, but was too weak to manage a smile. "It's okay. Don't be mad with her, and no I'm not, Cheryl Lee."

Cheryl Lee murmured an apology and left the room.

Wendy and Rebecca helped her onto the bed and then Wendy straightened Michaela's *kapp* and apron and retied the strings of her *kapp.* "There. You're good to go now."

"If you faint again you must go to the hospital to be checked out. Even if it's your wedding day," Rebecca cautioned.

Michaela nodded. "I will."

Hannah walked back into the room. "We're all ready and waiting for you, Michaela. How are you feeling."

"A little weird. I think I'll be okay."

Michaela and Wendy walked out of the room and out into the yard where the crowd waited. Wendy walked in front and soon Michaela was standing by Mervin's side in front of the bishop. Bishop Elmer had both Michaela and Melvin sit down.

"You okay?" Mervin whispered.

"Yeah, I'm fine. Just fainted but it was nerves, that's all."

He smiled at her and nodded and then when the bishop spoke, they both gave him their full attention.

When Bishop Elmer finished his talk, they stood up and the actual ceremony took place. Michaela tried to commit everything to memory like Abigail had advised. She especially liked the expression on Mervin's face when he looked at her. Seeing the softness in his eyes and the way they crinkled slightly at the corners, she was sure he loved her.

Then they were finally pronounced married; joined together in the sight of God. It was a moment that Michaela never really thought would come. Now all she wanted was to go home and be a family with Luke, but she'd have to stay amongst all these strangers who'd come from far and wide to bid them well.

Once they sat at the wedding breakfast table, Michaela told Mervin about Vera's letter. He sympathized with her about having no one there who really knew her.

CHAPTER 20

ANNE, Rebecca's sister-in-law, had kindly offered to look after Luke on the wedding night and Michaela had agreed. Rebecca had jokingly told Michaela that they might not get Luke back. Everyone laughed including Anne, who agreed she just might try to keep him.

Because Michaela was still feeling a little off from the fainting episode, the couple decided to leave the wedding early even before any of the guests had left.

As Mervin's buggy horse ambled steadily along the moonlit road toward home, Michaela looked over at her new husband. "It feels so strange without Luke and it'll be weird being without him tonight. He's been in my room every night since Lucinda left."

"Don't worry, it's our wedding night, our special night. It's the first time we'll spend the night together under the same roof as man and wife."

Michaela's nerves kicked in not knowing what to expect. Even Elspeth was staying the night at Hannah's home in the guest bedroom, so they could have the place to themselves.

When they reached the house, Michaela stayed close by Mervin while he unhitched the buggy and tended to the horse. Once he was done, he reached for Michaela's hand and she gave it to him. Together, they walked hand-in-hand toward the house, and he flung open the door.

"Let me show you what I've organized." He took her to a room and turned on the gas light. There was a crib in the middle of the room, lots of shelves for storage and a large chest of drawers. "Obviously, this is for Luke."

"It's *wunderbaar.* You've done such a good job." Normally when she'd stayed there on Friday and Saturday nights, Luke had stayed in the room that had been fixed up for her.

"Denke. Elspeth helped me organize it. It's not much now but at least it's clean and we can paint the walls to make it a little nicer."

"I can paint it in my spare time. I'll paint it creamy yellow and make new curtains to match. I'll make them in a heavy fabric to keep out the light so he can sleep better."

He chuckled at her enthusiasm.

"And, either side of his room, are our rooms."

The breath caught in her throat. *Our rooms?*

He stepped back into the hallway, opened one door and then another.

"We have two rooms? One each?" she asked trying to work out what he'd just said. She hoped he meant one of those room was a sitting room, perhaps a play-room, or possibly a sewing room?

"I thought it best to have Luke in between each of our bedrooms, so we can more easily hear him at night."

"Oh, we have separate bedrooms?" This is not how she wanted things.

"That's right. I thought that was best under the circumstances."

What circumstances? she screamed in her head. *We're married.*

She said nothing further in case she had somehow been mistaken. When she went into the room she'd stayed in on the last few Friday and Saturday nights, there was still a single bed there and the room was much the same as it had always been. "Nice," she said biting her tongue.

Excitedly he opened the closet. "And, you have plenty of space for your dresses. I cleaned out all the old boxes that were in here."

"I don't have much that needs to go in there."

"Then that should change. I'll buy you a whole bunch of clothes."

She giggled. "I don't need a lot."

"I want you to be happy and have everything you

ever wanted. If you want or need anything, ever, you just ask me."

"Denke." She looked around her room wondering how long it would be before they shared a room. There was one night stand and one dresser, blue curtains with fine white barely-noticeable stripes. "All right, show me your room."

He took her by the hand and led her to his room. It was pretty much the same as hers without the wardrobe. Again, there was a single bed. It hadn't even occurred to her that they would have a marriage like this, a marriage just for show. It reminded her of her own parents' marriage. They too had kept to separate rooms.

"Help yourself to anything you want in the kitchen."

"Jah, I will. I know my way around her kitchen and I know where everything is."

"It's as good as your kitchen now."

Taking things into her own hands, she closed the distance between them, wrapped her arms around him and tipped her head up, so he would have no choice but to kiss her. He blinked rapidly, then promptly gave her a quick kiss on the forehead. "Good night, Michaela, see you in the morning."

Embarrassed, she put her hands down by her sides.

When he turned and walked into his room, she was left standing there, rejected and dumbfounded. She stood there in shock for a moment, then walked into her room feeling like a big fool. After she'd closed the door behind her with her foot, she flopped onto the bed. Separate rooms and a kiss on her forehead—this was not how she'd pictured her first night of marriage.

A million things ran through her head all at once. Her head sank into the pillow and it wasn't long before her tears had saturated it.

When they'd decided to marry, she'd fooled herself into thinking marriage would solve all her problems, and she'd be loved and wanted. Right now, she felt more alone than ever.

"It's like he could've married anybody," she whispered into her pillow. "I should've gone back to Wiseman's Grove. Or even Wiseman's Valley, like Hannah said. That's right, I should've gone to a place that doesn't even exist, and who would even know I'd gone?"

SHE CUDDLED the dry side of her pillow and that gave her some comfort. The thought of Luke made her dry her eyes. She would devote her life to him, making sure he never felt the pain of being as alone as she was feeling now. When he grew up, she'd do everything she could to make sure he married a girl who loved him for himself.

At that moment, Michaela regretted her quick decision to marry a man who didn't wholeheartedly love her, but at least now she had a home. She remembered the words Vera had often said to her. *You have to make the best of what Gott gives you. He never stops watching to see who are going to be the faithful and trusting ones.*

Michaela decided she wasn't going to wallow in self-pity. She'd count all her blessings. She had a husband, and even if it was a husband in name only, at least she had one. Everyone in Pleasant Valley had been kind and friendly to her. She had women who had already befriended her, and she had a son. When she thought it through, she realized she was indeed blessed.

Not being able to sleep, she tiptoed out to the kitchen to fix herself a hot tea. While she sat drinking it, she hoped that Mervin might have heard her and come out to join her. Too upset to finish it, she poured the rest down the sink, and rinsed out her cup and left it on the dish drainer. Still in her mid-blue wedding dress, *kapp,* cape and apron, she walked back into her room and closed the door.

She opened her drawer and found a nightgown and replaced her wedding clothes with it before she crept into bed. Listening hard for movement in Mervin's room, she couldn't hear a thing.

CHAPTER 21

THE NEXT TIME she saw Mervin was when she was cooking eggs for breakfast.

"Good morning," she said as he pulled out a chair and sat down at the table. It was awkward to see him after she'd tried to make him kiss her last night.

"Good morning. You look lovely and fresh today after a late night."

"I feel good and I can't wait to see Luke."

"I thought we could spend the day together before we collect him. That is if you feel better today?"

"Oh, I feel fine and I was looking forward to seeing him as soon as we finish breakfast."

He chuckled. "I had a word with Hannah and she's agreed to keep him today, and she was arranging it with Anne. Between the two of them, they'll be arguing which one of them will look after him. Just for today. We can bring him home this afternoon."

"Okay."

He saw the disappointment across her face and he could only assume she wasn't interested in spending time with him at all. It was all about the baby. When he recalled their awkward moment before bedtime, it affirmed to him that she had tried to show some interest in him. "It was just an idea. We can collect him now and spend the day with him if you'd like. We can take him with us."

"That's okay, I'm just missing him. I'm used to waking up with him in the room and hearing his little smacking noises at night."

"It must've been strange without him. But you don't have to sleep in the room with him now that he has a separate room."

"I know." She then put the scrambled eggs onto two plates. "We have no bread to make toast. We'll have to pick some up today."

"By chance, you don't know how to bake bread do you?"

She laughed. "Of course I do."

"I'd love it if you'd make some."

"I can do it right now—if we've got all the ingredients?"

"We should have, but I don't want you to do it today. We have other more important things to do today. I've got somewhere special to take you."

"Really?"

He nodded. "It's a special surprise."

"For me?" she asked when she sat down opposite him.

"Jah."

"I don't need anything, Mervin."

"I think you'd reckon you'd need this. Just wait and see what it is."

"Okay."

As they sat eating breakfast it felt like the most natural thing in the world to be with him. The disappointment of the night before, however, wasn't far from her mind. She wanted to know what Mervin was thinking, but she wasn't about to ask.

THEY SET off in the buggy and he still wouldn't tell her where they were going. Then he parked the buggy and he led her into a lawyer's office. He sat her down in the waiting area and approached the receptionist. When he sat down with her, she was wiping away tears.

"Are you trying to get out of the marriage? Do you think that's what I want?"

"Nee, not at all." He frowned. "What would make you think that?"

The receptionist stood up, and said, "Mr. Abernathy can see you now, Mr. Breuer."

"Thank you." He stood up and then waited for Michaela to stand. Once she was on her feet, they both followed the woman into an office. “Have a seat. He’ll be in in a minute.”

When they sat down, Mervin told her, “This is about Luke.”

“Have you been in contact with Lucinda?”

“Jah I have, and she’s signed all the papers.”

“For … for us to adopt him?”

He smiled and nodded. “That’s right.”

She covered her mouth and tears filled her eyes for a second time that day. “I don’t know what to say.”

The lawyer walked into the office. “You don’t have to say anything. Just sign the papers.”

She gulped and looked at the lawyer as he sat down behind his desk. Then he pushed papers toward Mervin and told him where to sign. Then Mervin handed her the pen.

“Now, Mrs. Breuer, you sign on this line beside your husband’s signature.”

This was his surprise and it was the best one she’d ever had in her life. With her hand shaking, she scrawled her signature.

The lawyer leaned over and took the paperwork back. “Congratulations.”

“What happens now?” Mervin asked.

“I’ll file the papers and you two can get on with your lives with little … um,” he looked at the paperwork and read the name, “Nigel.”

“What?” Michaela bounded to her feet while Mervin did the same.

"It's Luke, not Nigel," Mervin grabbed the paperwork from Mr. Abernathy's hands.

The lawyer laughed. "I'm sorry. Just a little humor to start the day."

Michaela put her hand over her heart and slowly sat down, relieved and, at the same time, a little annoyed at the lawyer.

Mervin released the paperwork, sat down again, and patted Michaela's shoulder. "We'll get a copy of that?" he asked the lawyer.

"Yes. I'll get you a copy right now." He cleared his throat and walked out with the adoption papers.

"I thought we'd adopted the wrong child." Michaela giggled.

Mervin took hold of her hand. "Me too. I nearly had a heart attack."

"Denke so much, Mervin. This is my best dream come true. I don't know how you managed to keep it from me. I kept asking about Lucinda and now I know why you kept avoiding my questions."

"We'll leave this office as the parents of Luke, our son."

"And hopefully, we'll have many more."

He opened his mouth to comment, but with the worst timing in the world, the lawyer burst back into the office. "Two copies for you." He passed the copies to Mervin and before Mervin could take them, the lawyer pulled them away. "Or should I give them to your lovely wife?"

"I'll take them," Michaela said, reaching both her hands out.

They stood, shook the lawyer's hand, and then left his office.

"NOW, what would you like to do?" Mervin asked, as they walked back to the buggy. He hoped she wanted to spend at least a little time with him.

"It depends on you. What would you like to do?" She held up the carefully folded papers. "I've got the best thing I could ask for right here."

He chuckled. "How was that lawyer's joke?"

She shook her head. "It wasn't very professional."

"At least the job's done, and we're now officially parents."

"I know."

"Do you feel different?"

She stopped walking. "I think I do. I feel older and more responsible, and I can see you're already growing a beard."

He smiled as he touched his scratchy jaw. "It won't take long."

"This is the last day you've got off work, so you choose what we'll do."

"That's hard. I want to do something that'll make you happy."

She laughed. "You've already done that."

"I don't want to go home just yet, and I think we

should do something, just the two of us, before we get Luke."

"How about we go home and put these papers in a safe place and then we'll think about it?"

"Sounds like a good idea."

CHAPTER 22

WHEN MICHAELA and Mervin walked into the house, Michaela knew she wouldn't be happy until she told Mervin how she felt. She wanted to keep nothing from her new husband. "Can I have a talk with you?"

"Sure. What about?"

"About us."

He frowned. "Us?"

She giggled. "Don't look so worried."

"I am. It's always disturbing when someone says they want to have a talk with you."

"Let's sit down," she suggested.

"And it's something I have to sit down for?"

"It's nothing. Really, it's nothing."

"It must be something," he mumbled as he sat down on the couch in the living room.

She sat next to him and took a deep breath. "It's about our marriage."

"Go on."

"Well, it's … I just want it to be real."

"What are you talking about? Of course we've got a real marriage."

She sighed. He didn't have a clue what she was talking about. "Well, our first night together wasn't what I imagined."

"Now wait a moment. We both know why we married each other, so it's a bit late to start having second thoughts."

"I'm not, not at all." Now she didn't know what to say, so she sat there and stayed silent.

He ran a hand through his hair. "I don't know what you expect of me. The situation is awkward enough as it is and you've just made it even more so."

Now things were tense and she was only trying to make them better. "I was just trying to …" She sighed. "Don't worry."

"I can't help it if you don't like the way things are." He jumped up and stomped into the kitchen and she followed him and saw him gulp down a whole glass of water in one go. He then slammed the glass down on the sink.

"Careful. You could've broken it."

He spun around. "I don't care."

"You don't care about the glass or you don't care about me?" She folded her arms.

"I don't care about you? Not once yesterday did you ask how I felt. It was all about you and feeling sorry for yourself that Vera couldn't come and that *your* parents had died. What about me? Did you ever once remember that I have a *mudder* out there somewhere and she wasn't even at my wedding?"

She stared at him.

"Well? Marriage is a two-way thing. Stop thinking about yourself all the time. Stop talking all the time ... and ... and do more thinking."

She stared at him and her mouth dropped open. If he felt like that about her he should've said something before now. "You're horrible and mean and I wish I never married you." She stomped out the front door and closed it behind her. Not knowing where she was going, she quickened her pace to get away by herself. A lifetime of rejection flooded back through her mind. Everything was always the same and now it looked like her future would be no different.

"Wait, Michaela. I didn't mean it."

She kept walking. If he hadn't meant it, he wouldn't have said it. She walked on and on, worried about her future and most of all she was concerned about Luke. To give him a happy future they'd have to come to an understanding. She glanced around hoping he had followed and was ready to apologize. "He hasn't even bothered to come after me," she mumbled as she stomped over the gravel, kicking the larger stones as she walked. This was the first day of their marriage and it was terrible. All she'd wanted was to have an honest talk with him and he'd turned sour.

. . .

MERVIN WATCHED his new wife hurry away from him. She hadn't even come back when he'd said he hadn't meant it.

For the first day of marriage this was a very bad start. What did she want from him? He couldn't produce feelings that weren't there. And she knew very well the reason they had married was purely for Luke. "She knew what she was getting into," he told himself. He opened the door and called after her again, but she kept walking.

He closed the door and sat down on the couch. Remembering the bishop's words of yesterday, that the two now had become one, he knew he had to do something. She'd always been so happy and carefree. He had to make things right. He walked out of the house, and called out again, "Michaela!" but she was nowhere to be seen.

He jumped into his buggy, and hurried to find her.

MICHAELA WALKED on and on regretting saying anything to him just now. Eventually, she heard a buggy drawing alongside.

"I'm sorry, Michaela. I didn't mean to say that."

She stopped abruptly, and turned to face him. "*Jah*, but that's what you think, isn't it? I have to talk a lot because you never say anything. You don't tell me about yourself so how do I get to know you? That's right, you've got nothing to say now have you? You only talk when you absolutely have to. You have no conversation abilities. Didn't your parents tell you about conversation? How was I to know you were upset about your *mudder?* You only mentioned her once."

"I said I'm sorry. I don't know what more you want of me."

"Why would it matter since you don't want anything to do with me?" She turned and kept walking.

He pulled the buggy off to the side of the road and then ran to catch up. He jumped in front of her and placed his hands lightly on her shoulders. "I'm sorry, Michaela."

She pouted. "Why are you sorry?"

"It was cruel what I said just now."

"Did you mean it?"

"Sometimes you talk a lot and it's too much."

"I know because you don't talk. I have to fill the silence, or neither of us would say anything."

He nodded, knowing that was true—he hid behind a wall of silence, and she hid behind a wall of words. "I'll try to talk more. I really will. I want this marriage to work between us. I want us to have a proper marriage just like you want."

She looked away from him. "It doesn't seem like it."

Then they saw a buggy in the distance.

"Someone's coming. Quick, I don't want anyone to see us arguing. Get back into the buggy."

They both hurried to the buggy and it was then Michaela realized she was repeating what she'd detested about her parents' marriage. They fought all the time, but to the outside world they were a normal loving couple. That's not what Michaela wanted. "Who is it?" Michaela asked as the approaching buggy got closer.

"That's Hannah," Mervin said.

"She must be out this way to see us. I hope Luke's okay."

When they drew level with the buggy, Mervin knew at once something was wrong. Hannah had been crying. Panic struck him. It was his grandmother.

"Michaela, I have some bad news."

"Is my *grossmammi* okay?" Mervin asked.

Hannah looked over at him and nodded, then turned her attention to Michaela. "I'm sorry, it's Vera."

"What happened?"

"She died this morning. I wasn't going to tell you until tomorrow, but I thought you'd want to know as soon as possible."

Mervin looked at his wife and touched her arm. The disbelief on her face turned to sadness and tears streamed out of her eyes. This was something Mervin couldn't fix and he felt helpless, and awfully guilty for the argument they'd just had. It had been so unnecessary.

"The funeral's on in three days. I'll go with you if you want to go."

"How?" Michaela managed to say.

"An accident with a car. It was a blessing she went that way. It was instant. If she'd gone with the illness, she would've lingered."

Michaela put her head down and sobbed.

"Let's get you back to the *haus,"* Mervin said.

"I'll follow you," Hannah said.

Mervin walked with Michaela into the living room, sat her down and placed a blanket over her knees.

"I'll make you a hot tea," Hannah said.

"Nee, I don't want anything." Michaela picked up the adoption papers they'd left on the coffee table and clutched them to herself.

Mervin put his hand on them. "I'll put these in a safe place."

She looked up at him with pleading eyes. "Don't leave me, Mervin. Everyone leaves me."

"I'm just going to put them in my drawer with all my other papers. I'm not leaving."

She nodded. "Hurry back."

He walked to his room wanting to be more helpful in situations like these, but he didn't know what to do. Once he'd placed the papers on top of his other documents, he hurried back to see Hannah next to Michaela so he sat on the other side.

"We'll both miss her," Hannah said to Michaela. "But, we know where she is."

"It doesn't help. Everyone leaves." She looked at Mervin. "You won't leave me, will you?"

"Never. We're married."

"Don't die on me."

He chuckled, and then sobered. "I'll do my best not to, I promise."

Hannah told Mervin, "Michaela wants to go to the funeral."

"I'll go too."

"Nee, there's no need, Mervin. You've already taken time off work. I'll go with Hannah and take Luke."

Mervin nodded his agreement and realized he didn't feel comfortable that his wife was leaving so soon. They'd only been married a day and he wanted to make sure she knew how sorry he was about their argument. He had no idea where his sudden anger had come from.

"Elmer is bringing Elspeth back here soon."

"Denke. I could've gone to get her," Mervin said.

"It's okay."

"When are you thinking of leaving for the funeral?" he asked Hannah.

"Tomorrow."

He nodded. "Okay."

"Don't worry, Mervin. I'll make all the arrangements for myself and Michaela and I'll have her back to you in less than a week."

When Hannah left, Michaela asked Mervin to make a fire. She then sat there staring at it.

"I'm sorry, Michaela. Vera must've been very important to you."

"She was."

This was awkward. She was barely saying anything, and he wasn't used to trying to make someone talk. "Like ... like a second *mudder?"*

"Nee." She shook her head.

"What then?"

"I don't feel like talking, *denke."*

How could he help her if she didn't communicate? "Okay, I'll leave you alone. I mean, I'll be quiet. I'll just sit here close by and be quiet."

"Denke."

He sat in Elspeth's armchair, wondering what he could do to help. After five minutes, she was still sitting there in exactly the same spot staring at the fire.

MICHAELA HAD NEVER FELT MORE wretched. Now she had to sit in the house where she wasn't wanted while the husband who wasn't in love with her was talking with her and being nice. It was the very worst time for him to find his voice.

She wanted to yell at him and tell him if he didn't have feelings for her he shouldn't have married her, but they both knew the reason for the marriage and it wasn't love. She was stupid to hope that something would develop. Still, she wasn't going to argue and have a combative relationship like her parents.' It was better to remain silent. Yelling never really solved anything; she'd witnessed that time and time again.

Vera's death had brought home to her how short life was, and she'd left Vera. If she'd stayed, Vera might still be alive. Michaela had been the one to drive the buggy mostly, because of Vera's failing eyesight. Not only that, if she hadn't married Mervin, she just might've gone back to Wiseman's Grove.

"What are you thinking about?" Mervin asked.

"Just life and things."

"What things?"

"Life and death."

"Can I get you anything?"

"Nee, denke."

"When you're ready later we'll get Luke."

"Sure." Her thoughts turned to her son. If she'd never come to Pleasant Valley and married Mervin she wouldn't have Luke. She looked over at Mervin. "Can you get him? I'd like to stay here."

"Okay. Will you be all right alone?"

"I think so."

"I'll wait awhile."

She stared back at the fire thinking about her life and felt sorry that she wouldn't see Vera for a very long time. Her life had improved when she moved into Vera's home.

"You know, you're not the only one who feels alone at times."

Barely did she register what he said because she was

too lost in her own thoughts. "Is that right?" She didn't even look at him.

"It is."

Several minutes of silence had ticked by. He'd done his best to make her feel better by opening up a little—something he didn't find easy. "I felt alone when *Dat* died, and then even worse when *Mamm* disappeared. She left me without a care. I think I would've felt better if she'd died."

"I see," Michaela said.

By her response, he knew she wasn't listening. There was no point him even being there. He stood up. "I'll get Luke."

"Denke, Mervin. Are you sure it's all right that I go back to Wiseman's Grove for the funeral?" she asked.

"Jah of course. She was important to you. Go and pay your respects."

More than anything she wanted him to say he'd miss her or he'd be thinking about her, but there was nothing. To top it all off, he leaned forward and gave her a quick kiss on her forehead.

CHAPTER 23

THE NEXT DAY, Michaela was on her way to the funeral. She sat in a window seat of a train car, holding Luke close to her chest with Hannah sitting alongside. She'd learned Hannah had only once met her cousin, Vera, and only exchanged the occasional letter. "*Denke* for coming with me, Hannah."

"I'm excited to catch up with people. There are people I haven't seen in ages. I haven't been able to do this kind of thing for a long time. Now the boys are older, and I can."

"It must feel different now that they're growing up and don't need you so much anymore. I don't know if I can let go of Luke. I'll have to go to *schul* with him when he starts."

Hannah laughed at her. "I felt the same with my own but you get busier once the second one comes along and then the third and so on."

Michaela looked down at Luke and wondered what it would be like to have her own biological child. Would the love be different if she'd given birth to him?

Hannah interrupted her thoughts. "I know it's hard for you to leave so soon after you're married."

"It couldn't be helped." Michaela turned and looked out the window at the passing fields. There was a whole lot of empty space out there, with very few barns or houses. It looked lonely. Time away from Mervin might be good for her, but would he regret his hasty decision to marry?

To take her mind off all of her dark thoughts, she talked to Hannah about what was troubling her. An older woman such as Hannah might be able to give some good advice, she hoped. When Michaela finished her tale of woe, Hannah didn't look at all surprised.

"Believe me when I tell you it's not so strange."

"Really?"

Hannah nodded, and no hint of a smile touched her lips and from that, Michaela knew she was taking what Michaela just told her as serious. "Being the bishop's *fraa* I've heard every story and every reason for couples marrying. That's why I can tell you that what you told me is not as weird as you think. I'm not surprised about anything anymore."

Michaela gulped. It was embarrassing to talk about her feelings for Mervin, but no one occupied seats close to them so there was no risk of either woman being overheard. "I just want everything to be normal between us."

Hannah laughed, surprising Michaela.

"Have I said something funny?" Was there something Michaela didn't know?

"It's okay. Everyone takes their time getting used to one another and because of the way you came together it might take a little longer for you both to adjust to marriage."

"I just see everything he says and does as another rejection."

"You're going to have to stop thinking like that. You have to learn how to see the best, not the worst in life, and in everybody."

"I guess."

"I know you had a rough start in life with losing your parents and what happened to them and what happened afterwards, but that doesn't have to determine your future."

"But it kind of does."

Hannah pressed her lips together firmly. "It doesn't have to. Put it behind you and look at the way *Gott's* blessed you already. You have Luke, you have a husband, everyone in the community loves you and so does Elspeth as well. She's a dear sweet woman."

"I just want Mervin to see me as a real *fraa.* Do you know what I mean? Not just someone he married to give Luke a good life."

"Mervin's more confident and I can see the way he

looks at you—like he's concerned for you. I think he has special feelings for you that he probably hasn't even realized himself yet."

She hoped everything Hannah was saying was true and that she wasn't telling her things just to make her happy. Seeing as she had opened her feelings to Hannah and it had gone well, she decided to open up a little more.

"You know, Vera didn't treat me like one of her *kinner.* And I couldn't really expect to be treated like one of her own, but since she had taken me in, it would've been nice. Don't get me wrong, she was kind and everything and we really got along pretty well, and since my grandmother died she was the closest of anyone. But it just makes me want to treat Luke or any other child that might come into my care, with the greatest love I can."

"We're all *Gott's* children, and I agree with you. It shouldn't make a difference where the child has come from and whether he's yours or not."

Michaela felt her feelings were justified. That was all she needed to make her feel better. "I don't think I've even told you this yet, but we've adopted him officially. We signed the papers yesterday."

"See? That's another good thing to add to your list of blessings."

Michaela giggled. "That's right. I know everything you're saying is true. It sounds easy to do, but in the pit of my stomach I'm expecting everything to go wrong.

I'm expecting him to send me away and say he doesn't love me. Why would he? He never said he did."

"I suppose you think like that because you've had so many things go wrong and now you've come to expect it. You will have to practice every day when you wake up to expect the good."

Instinctively she put her hand to her mouth to bite her nails, but she caught herself in time, and then lowered her hand back to the baby. "I'll try very hard, because the other way's not a nice feeling."

"I can believe it. Give Mervin time. Don't expect too much of him too soon."

"Okay." After a while, Michaela glanced sideways at Hannah and saw her eyes closing. Feeling a little sleepy herself, Michaela settled into the seat and pressed her head back into the headrest. Second thoughts about sharing what she had with Hannah raced through her mind. She dismissed them. Hannah had given good advice, and she'd be used to keeping information to herself. After all, the bishop's wife couldn't go around blabbing everybody's secrets.

From the train station, they took a taxi into town and when they got there, Vera's husband was waiting for them. Being around Tom without Vera certainly felt strange. She didn't belong in this community anymore.

From the front seat of the buggy, Tom said, "Vera

was the happiest I've ever seen her when she got news you were getting married, Michaela."

"She was?"

"Tears came to her eyes and I never seen her cry for nothin' or nobody. She said you'd found your place. The place where you belong."

Hannah turned around from the front seat of the buggy and gave Michaela a big smile. Now she knew Vera had cared about her.

"That's a blessing to know. *Denke* for telling me." Luke started whimpering. "He's hungry. I'll have to heat up a bottle as soon as we get to your place, *Onkel* Tom."

"We've got a houseful. I've put you, Hannah and the little one in the same room. We borrowed a crib."

"I hope you didn't go to too much trouble, Tom," Hannah said.

"Nee, the girls did all the work."

ONCE MICHAELA WAS REUNITED with Vera's sons and daughters, she and Hannah went to their room to feed the baby his bottle.

Michaela sat on the bed with Luke while Hannah unpacked their clothes. "She cared about me, Hannah. In her own way."

"I heard. People have different ways of showing their feelings."

Michaela breathed out heavily. "It seems so. Maybe

she showed her love for me by sending me away. Letting me go, just like Luke's mother let him go."

"That's right."

Each day Michaela was away from Mervin, she missed him more and couldn't stop thinking about him. If only she hadn't tried to start the conversation that sparked that argument. She should've just let things be and allow things to take their natural course.

Three days later, they were back on the train heading home to Pleasant Valley.

CHAPTER 24

AFTER THE LONG TRAIN JOURNEY, Hannah and Michaela traveled to Elspeth's house by taxi.

Instead of Mervin being there to greet them, it was Elspeth who opened the door.

"How was it?" Elspeth asked with arms outstretched to take Luke.

"It was good, really good."

"Jah," Hannah said, "we both saw people we haven't seen in ages. It was tiring, but we managed. We stayed at Vera's home with Tom and Tom and Vera's unmarried *dochders.* There were so many people coming and going, and we were kept busy the entire time."

Michaela looked up at the house. "Is Mervin home?"

"Nee, he's not home yet."

"I'll continue on, Michaela." Michaela hugged Hannah goodbye, and when the taxi had driven away, Elspeth and she started walking back to the house.

"It was sad at the funeral, but we had good times there too."

"We all must go home to *Gott* sometime."

Michaela looked at Elspeth as she struggled to get up the two porch steps with the baby in her arms. "Are you okay with him?"

"I'm fine. Don't you worry, I won't drop him."

Michaela gave an embarrassed giggle. "That's not what I meant."

"I just can't do certain actions with my hands, but I can hold him. I might not be able to tie his shoelaces when I get older, though."

Michaela giggled. "We'll worry about that later on. Maybe he'll just have to wear boots."

Luke opened his mouth and gave little cries. "He needs a bottle. He slept most of the way." She put her bag down as soon as she got in the doorway and reached out her hands for Luke.

Elspeth handed him over, and said, "I'll put the bottle on for you."

"Are you sure?"

"Jah. I know what I can and can't do. If I need help with anything I'll sing out."

"Okay. I'll unpack my things. She placed Luke in his crib and hurried to unpack everything. When she'd gotten the main things away in drawers, she hurried back to his room.

"Bottle's ready," Elspeth yelled from the kitchen.

"Coming." She picked up Luke, who immediately

cried louder. "Bottle's coming. Don't worry." Seeing the bottle on the table when she walked into the kitchen she flopped down on a chair and then popped the bottle into his mouth. "I would've thought Mervin would be here."

While Elspeth rinsed out the saucepan she'd warmed the bottle in, she turned to look at Michaela. "He should be here soon. He wanted to be here when you got here but he had a bit of a problem with the buggy and had to hitch up the old one."

At that moment, they both heard a buggy. "Is that him?" Michaela asked.

Elspeth pulled aside the curtains and looked out the window. "That's him."

A couple of minutes later, Michaela heard the front door open and Elspeth left the room. Sitting there feeding the baby, Michaela had little choice but to stay put.

He walked into the room. The first thing she saw was his smiling face and then she noticed he was clutching the biggest bunch of flowers she'd ever seen.

"I've missed you both." He moved forward and in typical Mervin fashion kissed her quickly on her forehead.

"Are they for me?" she asked, looking at the flowers.

"*Jah.* I'll put them in the sink for now."

"*Denke.* I love flowers."

Once he'd put the flowers down, he looked over at Luke. "There he is, our boy. Has he been good?"

"Perfect. *Denke* for the flowers," she said again.

He pulled out a chair and sat down beside her. "I don't even know what your favorite flowers are."

"I really like them all. Anything, but yellow is my preference—yellow daisies, yellow roses. Daffodils ... pansies."

"I'll remember that. There are some yellow ones in there."

"It was thoughtful."

He stared at Luke. "I'm positive he's grown."

"Has he?"

"I'm sure he has."

"We've only been away for five days."

"It's been six. It's not been the same without you, Michaela. If you ever need to go anywhere again I'm coming with you."

She giggled, pleased to hear it. "Is that so?"

He nodded. "It sure is."

THAT NIGHT AFTER DINNER, they were alone again after Elspeth went to bed and Luke was asleep. They sat side-by-side in front of a romantic glowing fire.

"Tell me, why did you miss me so much?"

He frowned at her. "We only just got married and you left me."

She nodded, hoping for a better reason or some glimmer of hope that they might have a love-filled marriage one day. "I never told you, but my parents

didn't have a good marriage. That was why
myself that I should not marry. They put on a sh
the community, but inside the house there was t
all the time. They fought constantly." She looked
his eyes. "I don't want to have a marriage like that."

"We won't."

"Won't we?"

He rubbed his forehead. "What are you saying?"

"We had a big argument the first day of ou
marriage and when Hannah came along we acted as
though everything was fine."

"I see, and that reminded you of everything you don't want in a marriage."

"Jah and … *jah."* She nodded, not wanting to bring all her concerns up at one time.

"Is there something else?"

She shook her head.

He swallowed hard. "I don't even remember what it was about. We should never argue. I never want to."

"We're never going to agree on everything."

"That doesn't mean we have to argue about it. We'll talk things over, and then … and then we'll do things my way," he joked.

She slapped his arm lightly, and then laughed.

Then he said, "We're a family, and I'll do everything I can to make us all happy and healthy. I missed you when you were away. I've gotten used to you being around and I don't want that to ever change." He put his arm around her shoulders and she nestled into him.

sed her on her forehead. She wasn't anymore. One day soon he might kiss hat was her secret hope.

what our argument was about."

pered. "Let's just sit quietly and listen e."

was selfish."

his eyebrows. "I'm sorry, Michaela. I e not selfish."

k I was. I didn't even … it didn't even enter d that you'd be missing your folks at the ng. You were right—I was thinking only about elf."

"How many women would marry me?" He chuckled. "I'm a blessed man that you saw something in me worth taking a risk on."

She laughed. "Many women would've, if you didn't hide away here in this *haus.*"

"Well, I'm happy you came along when you did."

Pulling away from him slightly, she said, "You are?"

He nodded. "I know we didn't have feelings of love when we married and we married for other reasons, but now, I don't know what I'd do without you."

Her fingertips flew to her lips. "Really?"

"On our wedding day I looked at you and knew I was falling in love for real."

She remembered the way he had stared at her. "I'm feeling the same."

"You don't have to say that."

She giggled. "I'm not just saying that. I've not been able to stop thinking about you for a long time. Way before the wedding."

He smiled and tears welled up in the corners of his eyes. "This was all meant to be, all of it. Right from Hannah asking me to take a shy man called Michael to the volleyball."

She added, "Not only that, *Gott* gave us Luke."

MERVIN BLINKED RAPIDLY to try to stop the tears falling. He didn't know exactly when he fell in love with this incredibly annoying woman, but now he never wanted to be without her. She was like a small fragile bird that chirped loudly, but only because it needed special care. He thanked God for choosing him to be her husband.

He summoned all the courage he could. "We have a problem and I've been trying to think of a solution."

"Oh no. What's that?"

He swallowed hard. "It's about your bedroom."

"What's wrong with it?"

"While you were gone, I decided we should use it as a playroom for Luke. I'm going to start painting it tomorrow and you can't sleep in there because of the fumes."

"Is that right? Then where will I ..." She looked at him with big round eyes.

"If it's not going to be too inconvenient, you might have to share mine."

"Oh."

"Starting from tonight."

She nodded and when he saw a smile hinting around her lips, he knew the timing was just right.

MEANWHILE BISHOP ELMER and Hannah were drinking hot tea after all their children had gone to bed.

"What's going on with Mervin and Michaela? You said they looked like they'd been arguing the other day," the bishop asked.

"Did I?"

"Jah and you said you'd talk to her while you were away and see what was going on."

Hannah took a sip of tea. "They're fine. *Gott* brought them together. I knew it. I just knew it. He's quiet, she's a chatterbox, and the two balance each other. The timing was perfect, too, for the sake of Luke."

Elmer frowned. "What does that mean, they balance each other? Together they produce the sound output of one normal person?"

"Jah, that's right."

Elmer shook his head at his wife's reasoning. "Love. I'll never understand it."

"As the bishop, you should. Love is patient, love is kind—"

"And longsuffering." He chuckled. "I never see

things the way you do. I would've thought they'd be a dreadful pair. That's what I meant."

"Being with someone far different from yourself brings excitement. It's the unknown. You know what, Elmer?"

"What's that?"

"I think the Lord wants me to do this."

"What?"

"I might be good at matching people together."

Elmer shook his head and let out a loud sigh, almost a groan. "I don't know about that."

"I saw it. I saw the two of them would be good together right from the start."

"Just don't do it too much and then I think it would be all right."

Hannah took a sip of hot tea wondering if that was how God would use her in the future. The next community event was the school teacher, Deborah's wedding to William. They'd had an unexpectedly long engagement because William was adamant about altering his house before the marriage. In turn, Deborah was waiting for a commitment from May to give her six months substitute work at the school because Deborah wanted to be a housewife and homemaker for those first months while she settled into being mother to William's two girls, Ivy and Grace. Now they were ready for their nuptials. At their wedding, Hannah would see who was lonely, single and in need of a spouse.

AMISH WOMEN OF PLEASANT VALLEY

Book 1 The Amish Woman and Her Last Hope

Book 2 The Amish Woman and Her Secret Baby

Book 3 The Amish Widower's Promise

Book 4 The Amish Visitors

Book 5 The Amish Dreamer

Book 6 The Amish School Teacher

Book 7 Amish Baby Blessing

Book 8 Amish Christmas Wedding

Amish Women of Pleasant Valley Boxed Set Books
1 - 4

Amish Women of Pleasant Valley Boxed Set Books
5 - 8

~

ABOUT SAMANTHA PRICE

USA Today Bestselling author, Samantha Price, wrote stories from a young age, but it wasn't until later in life that she took up writing full time. Formally an artist, she exchanged her paintbrush for the computer and, many best-selling book series later, has never looked back.

Samantha is happiest on her computer lost in the world of her characters. She is best known for the Ettie Smith Amish Mysteries series and the Expectant Amish Widows series.

www.SamanthaPriceAuthor.com

Samantha loves to hear from her readers. Connect with her at:

samantha@samanthapriceauthor.com

www.facebook.com/SamanthaPriceAuthor

Follow Samantha Price on BookBub

Twitter @ AmishRomance

Instagram - SamanthaPriceAuthor

Made in the USA
Monee, IL
09 February 2023